Matilda Cha

Taken upon Trust

SALZWASSER
VERLAG

Matilda Charlotte Houstoun

Taken upon Trust

Reprint of the original, first published in 1863.

1st Edition 2022 | ISBN: 978-3-37500-210-7

Verlag (Publisher): Salzwasser Verlag GmbH, Zeilweg 44, 60439 Frankfurt, Deutschland
Vertretungsberechtigt (Authorized to represent): E. Roepke, Zeilweg 44, 60439 Frankfurt, Deutschland
Druck (Print): Books on Demand GmbH, In de Tarpen 42, 22848 Norderstedt, Deutschland

TAKEN UPON TRUST.

TAKEN UPON TRUST.

BY THE AUTHOR OF

"RECOMMENDED TO MERCY."

IN THREE VOLUMES.

VOL. II.

LONDON:

1863.

CONTENTS OF VOL. II.

TAKEN UPON TRUST.

CHAPTER I.

OLIVE'S STROKE OF BUSINESS WITH THE DWARF.

THE effect of Olive's nightly cogitations was to convince her that any attempt—for the present at least—to shake off her reputed father's yoke would be impolitic in the extreme. Though not what is generally called a clever woman, she was by no means destitute of the useful quality denominated 'sharpness,' and by virtue of that possession she discovered that her best chance of circumventing Redfern's schemes lay in his remaining under her own observation. It was rather a difficult task, she feared, to avoid exciting some suspicions in the invalid's mind when her change of purpose should be known;

and she laid awake for hours, meditating on the most efficacious way of avoiding those suspicions, and also of discovering the hidden springs by which he worked his dangerous and evidently complicated machinery.

To worm herself into the confidence of Redfern's tool and slave—for such she deemed the dwarf to be—occurred to Olive as the easiest way to reach her ends. To be sure, he was a vile and hateful-looking creature, added to which the words he used, and which she had overheard that night, were worthy of the degraded being by whom they had been spoken; but Olive had not been brought up in a school which fostered feelings of fastidious delicacy, and was therefore little likely to be deterred from an otherwise promising line of conduct, by yielding to any puerile sentiments of repugnance. She resolved then—but with a due regard to appearances—to make acquaintance with Master Amelius Driver, and try her hand, without loss of time, upon that ingenious young gentleman's weakest points of character.

It was, perhaps, fortunate for the success of her designs that, whether from the effects of over-excitement, or owing to a dram brought to him by the accommodating Yussy, Redfern's fever had considerably increased when Olive stood by his bedside on the following morning.

Common humanity formed an excellent pretext for Olive's apparent forgetfulness of her last night's threat, and it was with considerable inward satisfaction (heartless as the fact must cause her to appear) that Mrs. Gerald watched the wandering eye, and listened to the bald, disjointed talk which held out hopes of the betrayal of his secrets.

She brought her work—for Olive's habits had grown more womanly in her poverty and loneliness—and took her place behind the sick man's curtain. Her ears were stretched to hear the slightest sound, and soon her attention was rewarded by the seizing on what seemed to her an all-important clue.

'You mustn't tell your mother—not a word. I'll split your tongue, you little villain, if you do;' and then it was—'She thinks herself confounded clever, but I'll be more than up to her, the jade! She thinks she's found out about Carry. I say, Yussy, you young blackguard, don't you ever talk a word to Mrs. Bernard—mind now, if I catch you, you'll remember it. She mustn't know your mother's name is Caroline. She mustn't know—' but here the sick man's mutterings grew more low and indistinct, and after awhile he sank into a troubled slumber.

The sun had sunk behind the houses, and evening darkness was beginning to mingle with the London smoke, and still the sick man slumbered on, whilst the woman to whom he had unconsciously betrayed his secret kept her eyes fixed upon his heavy face unceasingly.

At last a step upon the stairs was heard by

the ever-wakeful attendant, and Olive rising stealthily from her chair, approached the door with noiseless steps, and with her finger on her lip. She looked out eagerly from the landing, and seeing Yussy on the stairs, she softly closed the door behind her, and descended slowly towards him.

'He is fast asleep,' she whispered. 'Come in here,' and drawing him into the little parlour, she motioned him to be seated.

There was scarcely light enough to see her face distinctly, but to the boy, whose memory recalled her features, as he had once seen them in the obscurity of night, she looked very beautiful. And hers was precisely the class of beauty which is appreciated by the coarse in mind and feeling—the kind, too, which, to a young lad of Yussy's temperament and age, appears as that of an enchanted goddess, to be gazed at, worshipped, and obeyed. She sat down opposite the lad, and fixed her eyes upon the face which grew quite red with unaccustomed shyness, as that handsome woman looked upon it.

'You have a message, perhaps, for Mr. Redfern?' she inquired. 'He cannot see you now, but you can trust me with it.'

'Thankee,' said Yussy, sheepishly, 'but, you, see I wasn't to—'

'That was only probably in case Mr. Redfern was well enough to see you, which unfortunately he is not. He is very ill indeed to-day; so ill that I must write to some of his relations, and I even think that he had better see a clergyman.'

'He sent me out to-day, marm, to try to get a something for him; and I wish you'd jest be good enough to say I couldn't get it.'

'Certainly I will; but won't you have a glass of wine before you go? It is very cold, and probably you have a long way to walk.'

Yussy accepted the offer gratefully, and in the course of the refreshing meal of cake and wine which Olive spread before him, he confessed to his far-away residence in Short's Gardens; and to the fact that he was precious tired with tramping all the day afoot, and wished old Redfern anywhere for letting him into such a shy concern.

Olive felt infinitely disgusted at the boy's familiarity—a familiarity which was only to be accounted for by circumstances, the existence of which Mrs. Gerald for the first time began to suspect. She was not the kind of character to bear patiently anything which she felt or suspected to be insolence; but if this—to her—revolting dwarf were in reality what she dreaded to imagine possible, then his detested free-and-easiness was scarcely to be wondered at. She was constitutionally and from habit an enemy to suspense, and therefore led at once to a subject that was likely to enlighten her.

'Your mother lives in Short's Gardens, does she not?' she asked.

'How did you know I'd got e'er a mother?' demanded Mr. Driver, with a cunning leer.

'Oh, Mr. Redfern told me, and he called her "Caroline"; he said he thought I ought to go with you and see her.'

'Well, that's a rum go, now,' remarked the lad, musingly. 'I thought that he was just the other way. There isn't much to see, ma'am, in my mother; she's precious slow, and almost always a crying; but I'll give your love to her all the same. You're Mr. Redfern's daughter, arn't you?'

'You are mistaken. I have nothing whatever to do with Mr. Redfern, nor is he in any way related to me. But I have some reason to believe,' she added, with an assumption of dignity which for the moment quelled her companion's insufferable audacity, 'I have reason to believe that I had once some acquaintance with your mother, and I have a great wish to see her and judge if I am not mistaken.'

'Well, mum, you can do that; you can come to our place, or you can go to market, or to church—not to the theaytre—mother's too religious by half for that; but in all them other places you can take a good look at her for nothing.'

'But I have no wish,' said Olive, remembering the boy's greed of gain, and acting on the hint, 'I have no wish to give trouble without giving something else besides. I want to see your mother soon—to-night if possible; but I am most desirous that she should know nothing of me or of my wish. Say, boy, can I trust you? Here, take this money, it is not much, but I can afford no more; take it, and keep my secret.'

She placed a bright gold sovereign in the boy's ready hand, and then continued thus—

'Let me go at night when she is asleep, and look upon her face. If she is my sis—my friend, I mean, one glance will be sufficient; but there are important reasons why your mother must not know that I have seen her. Say, are you willing to accept the bargain, and to conduct me in secret to your mother's side?'

'I'll do as you like, of course; but mother's mortal sick-looking in her night-cap. And if you screams out, marm,—why, what shall I do then?'

There was something elfish and uncanny in the boy's voice and manner—something even that struck Olive as bordering on insanity in his eccentric words. She thought this for a moment, but then the idea occurred to her that Amelius was playing a part, and affecting oddity to screen his real motives. This mental decision reassured her, and she no longer hesitated to carry into execution the plan which she had formed.

'At what hour do you usually return home?' she inquired.

'I haven't no particular times; I goes and comes like the swallows, and no questions asked.'

'I should like to go home with you,' said Olive. 'I mean after ten o'clock, when the house is quite quiet, and Mr. Redfern settled for the night.'

'You haven't got no character to lose, I reckon, or you wouldn't be seen so late with a young man as isn't from the country,' said Yussy, with an ugly laugh which showed his blackened teeth, and sent a shudder through Mrs. Gerald's strong-nerved frame.

He was certainly awfully unnatural both in looks and conversation; and a bolder woman even than Olive might have been excused for refusing to trust herself alone with one so impish. But Mrs. Gerald had a point to gain, and did not flinch in her resolution; so it was settled between the two that on that evening, Olive should leave the house when Redfern would least suspect her purpose, and, accompanied by Yussy, should proceed to Mrs. Driver's lodgings.

Redfern awoke refreshed from his long slumber, and bore better than could have been expected, Yussy's announcement of his temporary failure.

'I couldn't get a sight of anything to-day,

he said, when he and Redfern found themselves alone. 'The desk was never opened once, for the darned old fool had got the ear-ache, and Mother Grayton put an inion in his head so hot that he cried and bellowed like a good 'un. Lord, how he did hallo. It was as good as any play.' And Yussy laughed heartily at the recollection of the sufferings caused by worthy Mrs. Grayton's inadvertence.

'Never mind. It can't be helped. But you must keep your eyes open, and hope for better luck next time,' said Redfern, as he turned himself round in the hope of courting successfully another season of repose.

After the account that has been already given by Carry Driver of the vision that she saw in the stillness of the night, it is perhaps scarcely necessary to state in words that Yussy proved faithful to his promise, and conducted his new ally and benefactor to his mother's house in Short's Gardens. So long a period had elapsed since Olive had seen the half-sister of her childish affections, that but for the corroborating testimony which she had already collected, even the dark line of eyebrow, and the peculiar low, flat forehead of the sleeping woman would have failed to convince her that the changed woman lying on that miserable bed was in reality the light-hearted and loving playmate of her childhood.

She gazed at the poor changed, wearied face till her eyes grew dimmed with tears; but as she turned to go, Carry moved uneasily on her pillow, and one look from beneath her half-closed eyelids revealed to her the lovely vision of one on whom the grave long since had closed. She uttered a faint scream, and Olive, who had no present intention of revealing herself to one whose tie of relationship to herself was now no pleasant thought, hid herself behind the curtain, and with noiseless steps left the room where her momentary presence had caused so much surprise and consternation. It remains to be seen whether Yussy was ultimately successful in obtaining surreptitiously from Mr. Grayton the much-coveted paper; and also to what extent the lad was in reality the tool of those who thought to use him for their own selfish ends and purposes.

CHAPTER II.

COUSIN CHRISSY IN CLERKENWELL.

As I have not described Marian Clavering as that unnatural thing—a hard woman, the reader will scarcely be surprised to learn that, after poor Olive's hurried leave-taking, a gradual reaction took place in her feelings towards her sister-in-law.

She sat for a few minutes gazing at the empty chair in moody and self-reproachful silence: and then, yielding to a sudden impulse, she threw open the window, and looked out into the night. The cold was so intense that it almost took away her breath as, shading her eyes with her hand, she peered into the snow-lighted scene before her. The trees stood thick about the house, and, leafless though they were, their shelter was effectual in shutting out the first feeble rays of the early moon as the pale planet slowly rose to do her nightly duty. There was no wind—but only a silent, pitiless frost, so intense and piercing, that Marian, as she closed the window after her brief survey, awoke fully to a sense of her own cruelty in allowing her visitor to go forth alone and unprotected to dare the dangers of that dreary journey.

A sleepless night, and one of perhaps exaggerated forebodings, followed for Marian on that trying evening; but with the earliest dawn she rose, and startled her attendant with the information that she was about to proceed at once to London. The lady's-maid to whom this unexpected announcement was made, could not be considered as a favourable specimen of her class. She was a hard-featured and sharp-voiced woman; one, too, as her fellow-servants frequently noticed, who was very rarely beguiled into that natural expression of feeling, called a smile. She did her duty thoroughly in every department, and was never absent from her post, so that Marian could find no legitimate cause for displeasure against one whom, nevertheless, she could not help regarding with a singular mixture of distrust and aversion. Now also it occurred to her, for the first time, as a remarkable fact, that it was to Olive's recommendation she owed the possession of this, to her, highly-unsatisfactory domestic; and for no actual and assignable reason she found herself watching with some degree of curiosity the countenance and demeanor of the redoubtable Mrs. Dawson.

That their gentle mistress lived habitually under the yolk of her upper servants was a fact that those autocrats were perfectly aware of; and it was therefore a cause of some surprise in the household, when Mrs. Clavering manifested symptoms of revolt from their authority.

'I assure you it's no manner of use talking to her,' said Mrs. Dawson to the coachman, who had sent up his fiat to the drawing-room to the effect that he couldn't think of taking out his horses so early in the snow. 'It's no manner of use talking to her. I told her the horses would be *ball'd* with the snow—just as you said I was to—but she wouldn't listen to a word I 'ad to say. "You tell the coachman," says she, as up as may be, "that go to town this day I will—and, what's more, I shall go by the Ten train—so he had better be ready.'"

'Well, it's 'igh time Master was at 'ome again, if this kind of thing's to go on,' remarked the coachman, sulkily. 'My 'osses won't be worth a d— to-morrow, and so you may tell her: and she'll have a precious job, I know, to set it right with Master, when he comes to know it.'

But, notwithstanding the warnings of the stable authorities, Mrs. Clavering found the perils of the way by no means insurmountable; and on her arrival at the small wayside Station, was in some degree reassured concerning Olive's fate by the details given her by the station-master of that wilful wanderer's adventures during the previous evening. To be sure, she must have had a wretched walk, and then her fainting was of course an evidence of suffering and fatigue; but the lady had left, according to her informant's authority, in good spirits, and looking quite 'hearty.' So Marian, who, in truth, was little given to look at the occurrences of life in a gloomy point of view, pursued her journey with a lightened heart.

It had been her original intention to proceed at once to the Ranelagh Street lodging, and inform herself without delay of Olive's actual condition; but the more she reflected on that step, the more she felt comforted by the conviction that it had now become an unnecessary one. With her fears for Olive's safety, her kindly feelings towards that unfortunately-situated young woman had in some degree evaporated: and Marian, as she reflected on her own connection with the *ci-devant* Isabel Forbes, began to tremble at the idea of being brought into juxtaposition with any members of that decidedly unpopular family.

The result of this modification of feeling towards Olive was nothing less than a resolution, on Marian's part, to break through one of her husband's most authoritatively-uttered commands, and pay a visit to poor Cousin Chrissy in her prison. To do this, it was of course necessary for one (who was quite in the dark as to the measures to be taken in such a case) to drive first to Susan Brigham's lodging—a proceeding which, as it was also at variance with Mr. Clavering's expressed wishes, Marian performed by stealth and tremblingly. She had no difficulty in finding her friend's abode (which was, indeed, a wretched one enough), for Ernest Audaine had been the means of constant communication being carried on between them; so that Susan, although they had not met since the memorable night which followed on the Inquest, had never for a single moment felt that Marian had either neglected or forsaken her.

'You poor darling!' cried Mrs. Clavering, the moment that, freed from Susan's close embrace, she recovered from her emotion sufficiently to speak coherently. 'You poor darling! I have come at last to look at your dear, altered face,—and I know by *that* and by your weeping so, how much you have suffered! Why, Susan—you were once so very brave. Your Cousin Alick says you bore up so courageously at first—and, now--look up, poor child! your very cheeks are wan with all the tears you must have shed.'

Susan half smiled—a sad and wintry smile it was—at Marian's mistake.

'You have but small experience, Marian, dear,' she said, 'in this our woman's luxury, if you cannot see that this "good cry," as it is called, is an unwonted comfort. I never can, and never do, indulge in sorrowing with *her*, for everything depends on keeping up her spirits, and if she should imagine that

—that anyone, in short, she loves, is grieving; the poor soul frets so, that her health gives way, and nothing we can say has power to comfort her.'

'Yours is a hard task, dear Susan; but you have a sure reward, not only in your power of affording consolation here, but in the hope of a more certain recompense hereafter.'

'A recompense for what?' asked Susan, bluntly. 'For a simple, and, alas! I fear, a very inefficient discharge of a most sacred duty? For having at last discovered what a mean, selfish, cringing thing I am? For having—'

'Oh! Susan,' broke in Marian hastily, 'how can you say such dreadful things about yourself? How can you so belie your heart and motives? I shall lose faith in everyone if you shake my trust in you, whose conduct—nay, you shall not stop me, love—has ever seemed to be an example of a godly life.'

'The reputation for excellence is easily attained,' retorted Susan gloomily, 'if I have been fortunate enough to gain it; but, Marian, by those that look, as I have lately done, into the dark and unswept corners of their own black hearts, there are at times discoveries to be made which boldly speak against their undeserved fame, and make them feel their worthlessness.'

'My poor, dear Susan! You have grown morbid and melancholy in this lonely place, and with such heavy cares upon your heart. We have all been wrong to leave you so much to yourself, and I for one shall try and make up for the mischief that has been done.'

Susan shook her head mournfully.

'I cannot quarrel with my solitude,' she said, 'for it is to that I owe my knowledge of myself. Marian, you cannot imagine—you, whose life has been so uneventful, and whose responsibilities have been so light—the heavy weight of guilt which weighs me down! You cannot picture to yourself the misery of tracing out the causes of another's sin in your own cowardice—in your own wicked compromising with your appealing conscience! Nor what it is to me to feel that it was once in my power, by revealing a shameful secret, to—. But I must put a bridle on my tongue, for to speak now would be worse than useless, and fearful consequences to many might follow on one unguarded word of mine.'

Marian looked with wonder at the pale, agitated countenance of one whom she had always seen so calm, and self-possessed even in moments of sore trial and affliction; and the conviction was strengthened in her mind that to the entire isolation in which Susan lived, was to be attributed the sickly fancy which led her to such bitter self-accusation. Impressed with this idea, she turned the conversation to Mrs. Fletcher, and to her patient endurance of her daily and nightly cross.

'Do you think, dear, that it would give her pleasure to see me?' she asked. 'I would not go even to inquire after her till I had asked you; but if I know her well, poor thing!—and indeed I think I do—she is not one who would attribute my visit to an idle and childish curiosity; but still, she cannot know how deeply I have felt for all her sorrows, and how gladly, were it in my power, I would alleviate them.'

'You are right,' said Susan, 'in believing that Cousin Chrissy could scarcely imagine any but a good intention even in those who are her enemies, for she is herself so single-minded, that the possibility of a double motive would never occur to her. And Marian, it will do you good to see her! Now, perhaps you picture her to yourself as gloomy, tearful, and repining; but when you look across that dismal grating into the bare and whitewashed cell, and see that placid face, with its mild, trusting look of perfect peace, you will remember it, as I do, in your dreams, and say how true are the holy words of Scripture, that "God loveth those he chasteneth," and that "they shall know no evil whose minds are stayed on Him." '

'It must be a blessed consolation to you, dear Susan, to see her so resigned,' said Marian, in a broken voice.

'Hardly a complete one, for I cannot but have strange misgivings that there is the happy satisfaction of self-martyrdom in Cousin Chrissy's almost superhuman patience, and when that thought occurs to me my path of duty seems more beset with difficulties than ever. But, Marian dear, the time is slipping by, and this is the hour for my daily visit. If you desire it then we will go together, and after the expiration of the twenty minutes which the law allows for every visitor (and which I shall employ in preparing the poor prisoner for her interview with you), I will send to the Matron's room and tell you she is ready.'

The walk to the House of Detention was

a short one, and neither of the friends felt much inclined to break the silence, which lasted till they arrived at the Prison-gates. Marian's heart sank within her as she looked up at that gloomy entrance. It was her first introduction to a prison, and she glanced with wonder, not unmixed with admiration, at the cool self-possession with which Susan knocked at the gate, and addressed the officer who answered her summons.

'Visitors for No. 84,' said one official to another who came forward to accost them; and Marian shuddered to think that poor Cousin Chrissy's identity had already become merged in the two numbers which stood in large characters above her cell. They were at the door of her prison-chamber now; and Marian, at the invitation of the Matron, followed her into her private apartment.

'You will not have long to wait, ma'am,' said the head warder. 'Twenty minutes soon go—as, I dare say, these poor people often think; and Mrs. Fletcher is not very strong, and her voice soon gets tired of speaking through the bars.'

'Does she walk out at all?' asked Mrs. Clavering, who felt her heart swell with pity as she contrasted Mrs. Fletcher's present existence with the comfortable home she had once shared with the light-hearted girls she called her daughters. 'I hope she can still take exercise. It must be such a blessing to get out into the air; and, perhaps, there is a garden to the—the prison.'

'There is the exercising-ground, ma'am—would you like to see it? It is quite empty now, as the prisoners never walk except in the regulation-hours, and you will have plenty of time to look round before Miss Brigham returns.'

Marian accepted the offer, for she could with difficulty suppress her emotion; and the *tête-à-tête* with Cousin Chrissy's father formal-mannered guardian was gladly exchanged for a walk along the vaulted corridors, and an inspection of the exercise-yard.

'And this is where she takes her daily walks?' asked Mrs. Clavering; 'here, with these towering prison-walls around her, and, I fear, from what you say, surrounded by the criminals who share her prison.'

'Not exactly surrounded,' answered the matron; 'the prisoners are under strict surveillance, and are not only never allowed to address one another, but are kept during their walk at such a distance from each other that any intercourse between them is impossible.'

'But it is dreadful to think of her as mixed up with the lawless and the vile! Dreadful indeed, and almost impossible to believe that she, so pure and good, should breathe an air contaminated by the breath of thieves and murderers.'

'We have no murder cases here at present, ma'am, with the exception of—of—the one you speak of. Indeed, we very rarely have, excepting for a week or so. They go to Newgate generally—as this one will sometime before the Sessions.'

Marian's distress increased as she listened to the name of that horror-haunted Dungeon-house, but she asked no more questions concerning poor Mrs. Fletcher's future destination, so painful was it to her feelings to hear the unhappy lady's position discussed in a manner so unmistakably business-like.

The matron, however, apparently anxious to beguile the time agreeably, continued to enlighten her visitor on the subject of the present prison-occupants: telling of young and miserable mothers who had sought a dismal refuge in 'the dark flowing river,' but found it not. For strong and willing hands had drawn them from beneath the black and gloomy 'arch,' and now a Prison's walls concealed their misery and shame!

Marian listened with deep and absorbed attention to some painful details of individual suffering which had come under the matron's observation, and was still under the influence produced by those gloomy histories when she saw, to her infinite relief, the approach of Susan along the corridor.

'I may go to her now?' she asked eagerly of the matron, for, in truth, she felt eager to escape from the oppressive moral atmosphere which seemed to emanate from the cells around her. 'I may go to Mrs. Fletcher now, ma'am, may I not? Susan, is she expecting me? And are you certain she can bear so much excitement as a second visitor might cause her?'

'You will not find her excited,' answered Susan, calmly. 'But, try, dear, to have a cheerful voice and face; for Cousin Chrissy is not changed by her misfortunes, and would, as I have already told you, fret in secret if she imagined that either friend or foe were suffering from a secret sorrow.'

Perhaps—for Marian was a coward, and little used to sights of human suffering—perhaps she had indulged a latent hope that she might be spared an interview for which she felt her courage scarcely equal. It was a craven thought, and one that made her shrink abashed before the calm religious look in Susan's eye, as the latter pointed in the direction of Cousin Chrissy's cell. A few moments brought Marian, in company with the matron, in front of No. 84, and then, the latter having retreated to a distance, the visitor was left alone with the accused.

Never till now — often and compassionately as Mrs. Clavering had dwelt upon Mrs. Fletcher's imprisonment—had she realized the horrid, naked fact till now. But that solid metal-strengthened door, with its small grated panel, through which no friendly hand could press the trembling fingers of their harmless, kind old friend—all this would have destroyed illusions, had she still indulged in any—and have made her feel at once that to be free is in itself a blessing beyond price!

She could not speak at first by reason of the choking sob that rose so thickly in her throat, but Cousin Chrissy saw the pale, fair face behind the grating, and said in her own soft voice—

'My dear—I cannot find the words to say what good this visit does me. Put your hand against the grating, dear—there, just as Susan does. So—I can feel it now. It does me good to touch it,' and Cousin Chrissy laid her thin fingers against the hard, cold metal, through which she believed, but it was only fancy, that they came in contact with a human hand. Marian could see distinctly the interior of that dismal prison-chamber—its bare white walls—its high and iron-grated window—its asphalte floor, and the poor bed for which there was but barely space upon the hard, cold ground. She saw all this, and for a mere passing moment felt pity overpowering in its intensity for the bodily sufferings and privations of that patient prisoner.

But another glance at the calm countenance, serene in its heaven-supported strength, showed her that her compassion was thrown away, for that Cousin Chrissy was as happy in that narrow cell as if she breathed the breath of freedom, and was treading once again the garden-walks of her own country-home in peaceful Western England!

> 'In that cold cloister's stillness and seclusion,
> By guardian angels led,
> Safe from temptation, safe from sin's pollution,
> She lived in peace, and hope.'

'Oh! Susan, dearest friend,' sobbed Marian, as, an hour later, they turned down a quiet street, and left the prison-gates behind them, 'it seems wrong to grieve for one whom angels must have visited in her prison, but the sight of that unutterable resignation has made me feel that God is scarcely just—or would *she* be where we left her, and I free to go where I will with your hand clasped in mine, and a dear child waiting for my return, while—'

But here Marian stopped suddenly, for alas! there was but one other blessing in her life which at that moment occurred to her as worth the mentioning; and that other being neither more nor less than the devoted, and as she hoped, life-long friendship of Ernest

Audaine, it was perhaps just as well that she abstained at that particular crisis from dwelling on the gift she prized so highly.

But Susan had been far too greatly shocked at the extremely unorthodox opinion uttered by her friend on the subject of providential interpositions, to have any present thought for minor mistakes.

'Marian, what have you said? You could not mean it. Your visit to that trusting Christian has indeed been thrown away, if you have failed to see a celestial benediction, "under the dark disguise" of this poor, fleeting sorrow; but,' she added, feeling by the pressure of Marian's hand upon her arm that the rebuked woman's heart was too full for words, 'I am wrong to lecture you on this, or any other subject, for what am I—a selfish, erring mortal—that I should preach in this overweening fashion to others?'

'Susan,' asked Mrs. Clavering, abruptly, 'why do you persist in accusing yourself of selfishness? I could more readily believe you capable of any fault than that.'

'Because I feel that I deserve it. Because I know that dread of personal discomfort—dread of incurring personal dislike—and above all, a mean and despicable pride, the nature of which you must know my most hidden weaknesses to understand, have been at the lowest root of all my actions. A year ago—what do I say?—a month ago, I should have resented it as an indignity had anyone dared to accuse me of self-concentration and self-seekingness, but now I see my character in its true light, and feel that there was selfishness worked up in every word and thought for which I claimed my own and others' praise.'

'But you always *seemed* to think of others,' remonstrated Marian.

'Of course I did,' retorted Susan, bitterly. 'That was part of my system. It was right for my own sake to think about my neighbours. Right for my own sake to dwell upon my own motives—my own conduct—my own example. Oh! it is terrible to think how self enters unconsciously into all our actions, and especially into those for which the world holds us up to undeserved admiration.'

'How hopeless you make me feel,' said Marian, mournfully; 'and how impossible it seems to keep our motives clear!'

'So I decided once, and when first the new view of my past conduct made me so clearly see my own intense unworthiness; but, dear, there is a remedy for this fell disease, and one — thank God! — within the reach of all of us.'

'And that one is?—'

'*Work* instead of thought, and active *practice* instead of empty theory. By dwelling upon what we *ought* to do, we lose the time which could be well employed in useful service for our fellow-creatures; and we learn to dwell upon our own entirely ideal perfections till we forget that there are others in the world besides ourselves. "Love thyself last!" So spoke in his last memorable moments a man who had earned by his own experience the right to give advice; and *I*, a humble, late believer in the truth, can bear my feeble testimony to the fact, that in forgetfulness of self, acquired by an active discharge of our duty towards our neighbour, lies our best chance of happiness.'

Unfortunately for the success of any projects which Susan might have formed of improving the moral condition of her friend, Mrs. Clavering was not as yet prepared by circumstances for the completion of her work. She had often been unhappy, certainly; often been convinced that life was nothing better than a burden, and that to endure existence was as much as could be reasonably expected of her. But notwithstanding all these gloomy and depressing convictions, Mrs. Clavering had never yet come in contact with the stern reality of suffering. She had been worried by her husband systematically—had been forced to shut within herself a thousand tender, womanly feelings, which the unsympathizing Leo would have contemplated with the ridicule which was, perhaps, their due; but, on the other hand, she had had her consolations—a fact which was proved by the still rounded cheek, the elastic step, and the infinite care which the pretty Marian still continued to take in her personal appearance.

No woman is to be pitied as long as she can look complacently in her glass and consider seriously the effect which her appearance is likely to produce on any man of mortal mould. When that feminine occupation has ceased to afford her pleasure, and when all that remains is to sit down amidst her ruined hopes, and watch the sure decline of all her powers of charming, then must a feeble woman own her weakness, and looking round her for some surer, safer stay, must bear in mind for her great comfort, that—

When the hours of rapture gay,
On the lone ear die quite away,
The lonely heart seems lifted nearer Heaven:
Seen daily, yet unmark'd before,
Earth's common paths are strewn all o'er
With flowers of pensive hope, the wreath of man forgiven!

CHAPTER III.

SUSAN KEEPS HER SECRET.

MARIAN found it very difficult to respond in a befitting manner to Susan's exhortation. She acknowledged to herself (for her judgment was less erring than her heart), that Susan's theory was correct, and her teaching admirable. Perhaps, too, had there been no such being as Ernest Audaine in existence, or rather if such a being had chanced to be unknown to her, the better, higher nature of Marian Clavering would have led her to yield herself at once a willing disciple to this new doctrine, and to enter with enthusiasm into the promised joys of self-denial. But situated as that still-benighted lady was, she deemed it more advisable, seeing that she could not enter warmly into the subject that had been broached, to turn the conversation to Mrs. Fletcher and her wrongs.

'I would have given worlds,' she said, 'to show her long ago that, although I could not really, truly aid her, I felt for her most deeply and sincerely.'

'She never doubted it, I am certain,' responded Susan. 'But, Marian, you are rich and prosperous, at least the world accounts you so, and perhaps—you see I can turn beggar for my friends—you might from your abundance save a little trifle towards our guiltless friend's defence. She is so very poor, dear Marian—we are all so poor—or you should have heard from me no word of this.' And Susan blushed beneath the thick folds of her mourning veil to think she should have stooped to ask for charity! Marian was by nature a generous woman; nay, her very weakness of character led her into the perils of extravagance, for she dreaded ridicule and censure, and dearly loved, though in no truckling way, the praise of men. It was therefore with a very bitter feeling of regret that she was compelled to admit her utter inability to come to Cousin Chrissy's assistance.

'I am poorer than even you can conceive,' she exclaimed, in the exaggerated terms peculiar to persons of an excitable temperament—'poorer in the midst of all my luxuries than even Cousin Chrissy in her gloomy prison. I have nothing that I can call my own—nothing that—'

But here her voluble assertions were cut short by Susan's quietly remarking that they had arrived at the end of their walk, and that perhaps dear Marian would come upstairs, and judge for herself of their comparative degrees of poverty.

They were striking contrasts in appearance, these two women; for whereas Mrs. Clavering's long and richly-flowing robes swept royally along the narrow passage, and more than filled up all its width, Susan's almost scanty garments, uninflated (if I may be allowed the expression) as those of a Sister of Charity, seemed well adapted to the dimensions of her tiny dwelling-place.

They had ascended three long winding flights of stairs before they reached the end of their wearisome ascent—an ascent which was terminated by a low, narrow door, the dark-coloured paint of which was worn off in places, showing unseemly patches of a dirty white, on which facetious visitors of former lodgers had traced their names, and even some their portraits, in various devices more comical than artistic.

The room itself, or rather attic, into which Susan ushered her visitor, was but little larger than Cousin Chrissy's 'special cell,' and was almost as bare of furniture. Marian looked around her in amazement at these signs of penury, and then throwing her arms around her friend, she exclaimed, with an overpowering outbreak of emotion—

'Susan! how could you let it come to

this? How could you keep us all in ignorance of your privations and your poverty? Ah! if I had known of this before, nothing should have kept me from you. I would have braved, as I have done now, my husband's anger, and have borne my part, as I will now in supporting you and *her* through all your trials.'

'Braved your husband's anger!' broke in Susan, hastily. 'Marian! you cannot mean that you are here against your husband's wishes? You cannot mean that he has refused his sanction to your visits?'

'He has, indeed; and that without a word of explanation of his motives. I bore it patiently, as I have done his tyranny and harsh injustice since the fatal day I married him. But last night Olive came with hints of coming misery for all of us, and she so wrought upon my fears that I could bear suspense no longer. She spoke of Florence—of my sister-in-law—and made me tremble for my brother's happiness.'

'What did she say of my poor cousin? Tell me all, dear Marian—every word and look, for this is very serious.' And Susan's voice faltered strangely as she spoke.

'Then there is some awful meaning in that woman's words! I knew it—I could have sworn it, although, indeed, she said but little.'

And on being again urged by Susan, Marian repeated to the best of her power all that she remembered of Olive's mysterious words.

Her cousin heaved a sigh of relief when her relation had concluded.

'There is, as you say, not much in this, but little as it is, dear Marian, be ruled by me, and keep it to yourself. Even to her brother you must repeat no syllable of what fell from Olive's lips. On one subject, and on one alone, can there be unreserved confidence amongst us, for in proving our dear friend's innocence lies the only chance of safety for others besides herself; and, therefore, for that end we must all work in concert. Mr. Audaine is in all respects our chief supporter, and when I tell you that he knows all, and more than all, than can by any possibility have come to Olive's ears, you will, I hope, be comforted, and feel that the interests of Florence and your brother are not wholly unprotected.'

A pang of jealousy—she could not help it — shot through Marian's heart at the thought that Ernest had kept a secret from her, — a secret too which he held in common with one who, though her beauty was dimmed and faded, still possessed many a youthful, womanly charm capable of touching a heart susceptible and warm as Ernest's.

'I am surprised,' she said, in a tone almost of pique, 'that Mr. Audaine should not think me worthy of confidence, especially in a matter involving family interests which he knows are dear to me.'

'He has done it for the best, believe me; and, Marian, the time may come—God grant it will not—when our motives for this secresy will be revealed to you. But till then, be patient, love, and trust to Him who alone is mighty to save, that He will mercifully guide us out of all trouble. Do not come again, dear,' she added, as she folded the thick mantle round Marian's graceful shoulders; 'let your husband's will, however hard to yield to, be your law, and trust to us that in this time of trial nothing shall be wanting to bring things to a happier issue than we can at present dare to hope for.'

Marian descended the dirty narrow stairs alone, reflecting as she went on this most unsatisfactory ending of an unsatisfactory interview; but long before she reached the end of her lonely journey homewards, she had definitively made up her mind that before many days were over she would have a satisfactory explanation with Ernest Audaine.

That her constant and usually unreserved friend should have not only received a confidence but kept a secret from which she was excluded, convicted Ernest in the eyes of his lady of the high crime and misdemeanour of *lèse-amitié*. And then, too, it was in concert with a woman, and that woman young, pretty, and invested with the interest of a great sorrow, that this treacherous plot against her peace had been carried on; and Marian, as she reflected on this exceeding aggravation, awoke to a clearer conviction even than before, of how necessary to her happiness was the possession of Ernest's undivided heart.

Truly this was neither a safe, nor a profitable state of mind for a wife who must prepare to meet the husband who, after a fortnight's absence, was expected at his home that day; but Mrs. Clavering was too much absorbed in other thoughts to dwell upon her more legitimate causes for anxiety; nor had she yet made up her mind as to the extent to which she should confess her disobedience to her tyrant, when the sound of that amiable autocrat's step in the entrance-hall recalled her from imaginary discontents to the endurance of real sorrows.

CHAPTER IV.

THE CURATE IS IN DANGER.

Lord Ashington, the object of the obscure but savage Redfern's hatred, lived in a fine house in Belgrave Square. It was a great stone building, with a massive portico, under which sick, wretched, homeless wanderers stopped for rest and shelter on December nights; and from whose broad white pillars (in the soft summer-time, when pretty ladies clad in satin came to the great house on gala-nights), another shelter stretched across the pavement, for fear the petted children of prosperity should have their cheeks too roughly visited by the winds of heaven. There was an enervating and luxurious air floating within and all about that lordly mansion; and a poor man—one whose life had passed in other scenes and places,—places where wholesome toil and sight of human suffering brought stern reality in bold relief against ideal beauty, might almost 'lose his head' at first, should fortune take him with a sudden lift to that enchanted palace. For its owner was a man of rare and exquisite invention, and with his wealth at will could summon pleasures to his princely home, and buy the worship which his age had else denied him.

There can be no doubt that long and constant enjoyment of enervating pleasures causes such pleasures to become as even the necessaries of life; and thus it was that old Lord Ashington had grown a slave to his own tastes and habits. He did not know, poor man, to what extent his senile weakness had become at once a mockery and a means to others, for he thought—the case is not uncommon—that pretty women came to see him for love of his fine person, of his gracious manner, and all the well-turned playful compliments which from the old man's lips they listened to so graciously.

So Ashington House (although its lord had lived there season after season till more than threescore years and ten had rolled above his head) was still the pleasant and the gay resort of thronging crowds of fashion—still the place where on a stated evening of the week, the world could meet the world, and every human being feel that he had done his duty.

For a long time, the question as to who would succeed to the vast wealth and mighty titles of the noble lord had been often mooted, for it was well known that the Right Honourable Earl had not one near relation, and the whisper had long since gone forth that the next heir was something 'very low.'

'Has stood behind a counter,—on my soul I heard so,' was the decision of an Honourable John, whilst little Charley Tufthunt, at the 'Rag,' declared he knew the man—'had seen him with some medals on, doing a commissionaire's work outside a shop.'

'A great, good-looking, strapping fellow,' so he said, 'was pointed out to me one morning by the Dook of C——. I thought it doosed odd, and should have questioned him if I had had a moment's time, but Thérèse was waiting for me in the Park, so hang it, I was obliged to cut.' And little Tufthunt having proved to his own satisfaction that he was on speaking-terms with a duke, and had an appointment with a fashionable actress, went on his way rejoicing.

Such were amongst the small *on dits* uttered by little people on the subject of that great Inheritance, whilst all the time a pale-faced, quiet man—a humble, seeming Christian, nothing versed in worldly ways—went plodding on his path of duty, his willing hand for ever on the plough, and never looking back through the long working-day.

It was not till a series of events had made Alick Harley's succession to his distant cousin's title almost a certainty, that anything was 'done' for the laborious, ill-paid

Curate, by the relations with whom gold was well-nigh a drug. He had but little worldly ambition, that same long-looked-over heir-in-tail, and very seldom in his arduous course of duty, nor even when tired, sick, and jaded, did thoughts of possible contingencies render him less zealous in his noble work. But still, when mighty changes came, and when sweet syren voices spoke to him in flattering tones, and bright eyes softened as they looked with pleading eloquence in his, then Alick, for the first time in his life, was greatly tempted, and not St. Antony with the demon's baits around him was more sore beset.

Alick Harley was a man who knew no middle-course between the bad and good. He could not temporize, or throw into one scale a make-weight, with the which to satisfy his grumbling conscience. But although at first he made brave head against the lures laid out for him, defying devil, world, and flesh, with well-girt loins and banners flying, the time arrived, although by slow degrees, when habit did what the first change had failed to effect; and the Christian pilgrim, whilst his conscience slumbered, began to estimate the luxury of being courted.

Lord Ashington would gladly have found amongst his distant kinsmen an heir a little different from Alick. He did not like the Curate's ways, his principles, or his profession. And as for manners! 'Why, sir,' the aged nobleman groaned out at White's,—'why, sir, you'd think he'd never seen a gentleman in all his life. A priggish parson, with a stiff white neckcloth, that looks the character from head to toe. And as for women! 'pon my soul, I think he couldn't look one in the face.'

'Set Louisa Graham at him,' said a younger man, who had caught the slang of junior members, and talked of London girls familiarly,—'set Loo Graham at him; that's the sort. Your shy men are so thankful to a fast young woman, that they fall in love, and speak of marriage in an hour after.'

'It's my belief,' said Ashington sententiously, 'that it's because men grow so much more dull than they used to be in my day, that the girls have become so forward. In my time—twenty years ago—the men did all the work, and our young ladies didn't seem to know the fact that through our senses we are easiest worked upon.'

'The sons of Adam haven't changed, I fancy,' put in the other colloquist. 'The women do beguile us still, and make us eat forbidden fruit. But how about Miss Loo?'

'She's a little old,' mused Ashington.

'Yes, and her parents hard as nails; a horrid lot, although they're my relations. But if I don't mistake, Louisa Graham has a pull; for she was first-and-foremost in the field, and I believe the Curate's spoony.'

'Impossible!'

'Not at all; I don't believe he's even difficult,—and if you make no objection—'

'Not I; I'd rather, perhaps, he'd marry something younger. But after all, there'll be an heir most likely; those curates always have the devil-and-all of children, and it is a good connection. She will form him, too.'

'*Form* him! I think she will! And as for Lady Annabella, if she doesn't squeeze him into a mould, and make him hard as cobler's-wax, I'll engage to marry the eldest daughter, and honeymoon at Tonbridge Wells."

'The eldest daughter's horrible,' said Ashington, who, after the fashion of the world, had no compassion for ugliness, save when it was joined with wealth or high degree.

'Poor Janet! she's the best of creatures, as ugly people ought to be. But tell me—have you heard the news? They say that "Vampire's" far ahead. I saw a telegram an hour ago, and Brading hadn't then a shadow of a chance.'

And so they gossipped on of politics and races—men and women, whilst Alick Harley, caught in Miss Graham's well-placed net, gave not one token of resistance, but lay a passive victim at the schemer's feet.

There was a large and brilliant evening party at Ashington House on the occasion when the engagement between its heir apparent and the daughter of Lady Annabella Graham was made known into the world of fashion. Of course, the younger ladies laughed and sneered, hinting that not for worlds would *they* have condescended to a man so vulgar, and whose exterior was so very much unlike the gentlemen with whom they came in contact.

And then he seemed so little to appreciate the privilege of admittance to their select companionship! He was not one of *them*—could never be, with his strict, foolish notions, and his manner, which was like nothing else that they had ever chanced to see. He hardly seemed to understand a single word they said to him, and only looked at home when Louisa—oh, that woman's art!—spoke of religion to him, and of visits to the sick. The scheming creature!

'Positively I've heard they've been together to some horrid places—into low courts and alleys—where the Curate used to go before Lord Ashington decided that he'd try to make a gentleman of him. I wonder that she's not afraid; she wouldn't like it if she caught a fever.'

'She needn't be afraid of *him* at any rate. What fun those pious people seem to have! They can do fifty things that wicked men must leave alone. Just fancy Colonel C—— or Lord Augustus taking Georgina Boyd or Miss Pendennis to lonely places *tête-à-tête!* Why, they would be the talk of all the clubs. They'd say—'

'Hush! Here she comes. How wonderfully she wears. You really would not guess her more than thirty-five. My dear Louisa' —kissing her with warmth—'I am so glad; he is so nice and good.'

'I am sure you will be happy. When is it to be?' cried equally demonstrative Number Two. And then they sat down in a corner, talking trousseau, jointure, diamonds

—but avoiding love, as somewhat out of place and season.

Louisa Graham had been an acknowledged beauty in her youth, and now, at five-and-thirty (which she did not own to) the world acknowledged her a handsome, showy woman. She had fine drooping shoulders and a lovely bust—a complexion which by day was rather thick, but in the glare of candlelight, and aided just the slightest thing by art, its brilliancy was striking. She was very clever—had been taught with care, and having lived from childhood in the world, had caught its jargon, and could talk it well. It was some years since this accomplished London lady first became acquainted with the then very doubtful heir to wealth and honour. He was a poor, pale student, passing, with his friend Audaine, a pleasant summer at the English lakes. Ernest had known him first, when Alick was a weakly boy, at college, and being much his senior, had taken pity on the lonely lad, whose childhood and whose youth had not been passed amongst kind friends and loving relatives. He had been sickly also from his infancy, and Ernest, deeming change of scene and fresher air would brace him into greater vigour, proposed, one season in the long vacation, that they should journey into Westmoreland together. The gratitude of the home-staying, shy, but nature-loving boy, was too intense for words, and if his friend had needed a reward beyond his consciousness of charitable deeds, he would have found it in the new spirit that seemed infused into the student's nature, and in the glow of health that soon became apparent on his sallow cheek. They took up their temporary abode by the least cockney-visited of those glorious lakes, and there, as they professed to come for study (there being a pleasant fiction extant to the effect that Audaine was reading for the bar), they laid in goodly store of books.

It was on a lovely evening, the closing in of a day which had been spent within the house, for a gentle rain—the 'Scotch mist' of the mountains—had fallen continuously till the sun had nearly set, when, following the invitation of the first long, slanting ray of light that beckoned to them through the latticed window, the friends laid aside their ponderous books, and betaking themselves to their little wherry, rowed idly from the shore. There was no wind, and the closeness of the atmosphere rendering exercise unpleasant, they ran their tiny craft alongside of a small wooded island, and there, resting on their oars, they remained for awhile in admiring silence—a silence that, to the one who was now for the first time realizing the long-panted-for joy of revelling in the beauty of mountain scenery, was sweeter far than music.

'Beautiful! most beautiful!' he exclaimed at length. 'And how passing strange it seems that men are found, eager to dwell in the great "graves of cities," when they can leave the polluted air they breathe in them for a heaven-bless'd spot like this!'

'We are probably better off here without some of the ghouls you speak of,' responded Ernest with a smile; he was but half romantic, and, besides, he wished to bring a healthier tone to Alick's mind. 'Yes; we are certainly better off without them—but, indeed, for that matter, I confess I know but few who would not seem most strangely out of place in this our solitude. As for myself, I don't pretend to be amongst the exceptions; for if respectable behaviour—past and present, and I fear to come—are qualifications for admittance, there can be little doubt that Ernest Audaine would be black-balled by all the spirits in these mountain solitudes.'

He laughed at his own nonsense as he gaily uttered it, and then, springing lightly from the boat, he reached the shore, with the intention, as he said, of exploring the interior of the island.

In a few minutes he returned, with his finger on his lip, and beckoning Alick from the boat, he pointed to an opening in the trees.

On a block of stone was seated a young lady—at least, as seen in that dim light, she might claim a right to be considered juvenile—and near her stood an old and patient-looking gentleman. The lady had her sketch-book in her hand, but she was doing nothing—only looking pretty and attractive.

'By Jove! There is Loo Graham,' whispered Ernest, 'but I need not speak so low—for she is not frightened easily. But what the deuce are she and the old General doing here?'

Ah! what indeed? But soon the man of worldly knowledge guessed the reason why in spite of dullness, rain, and poor accommodation, both for woman and for beast—(for General Boldero had his horses at the village, and all his niece's soft cajoleries failed to convince him they were well attended to)—in spite, I say, of all these many inconveniences,

Louisa Graham and her old good-natured uncle lingered at the 'Dacre Arms,' and made quite light of its inconveniences.

There was no reason, perhaps, why Audaine should feel that Miss Graham had designs upon his friend, but still he felt suspicious when she met him by 'mere accident' in his lonely walks, and smiled so blandly on his poor plain friend.

At that period Alick could hardly be called impressionable. Possibly, he was too sensible of his own personal deficiencies to comprehend the kind advances made to win him from his *sauvagerie.* But still, and all undreamt of by himself, he felt the charm of being petted by that handsome, talking woman; for Louisa Graham did make much of him, and in her pleasant coaxing way would try to make him bolder in his speech—more self-assured, and independent. To Audaine, the sight of the clever play, enacted on the greensward and on the bosom of the tranquil lake, was one that he could look on after awhile with unmixed amusement. He had no fear of Alick's heart becoming interested in the pleasant game, and only looked upon the talented Louisa as a means to free his friend from trammels cast around him by his morbid shyness.

After awhile he thought it would be wise to leave them for a time alone, and so, pretending urgent business (for well he knew that Alick's humble bashfulness increased in its intensity when *he* was present), he took his departure for London. What passed between the incongruous pair, when—one at least was left without a Mentor, and (for the General was but a 'cypherish' kind of chaperon) they might be deemed *alone*, was never talked of, even to the most intimate among his friends, by Alick Harley. More than three working years had passed away before he met again the woman whose alluring ways had first opened to the country-nurtured student a vista of future happiness, of which love would be the beginning and the end. Of how his mind and memory had clung and lingered on gone-by scenes of beauty when her soft touch had thrilled upon his heartstring, and her spirit-stirring voice had sung to him upon the silent waters, it is not needful here to dwell. He never called himself a fool for loving her, when weeks and months rolled by, and she had clearly lost all memory of the past. No—*he* had been no fool, for how could he or any man resist that syren voice (Alick, as we see, had grown poetical) and sweet persuasive manner? It was that *she* had been too lenient to his faults and too oblivious of his crying imperfections; and so when others—better, brighter friends surrounded her with incense and adulation, she could not but forget the obscure and poorly-gifted being, who in default of other and more acceptable idolators she had allowed to kneel before her shrine.

Meanwhile, and if the truth must be spoken, Miss Louisa Graham was not idolized at all. Her day, like that of many a better dog (we beg her pardon for this using of the proverb), was over, and dozens of younger, fresher beauties had since usurped her place, smiling the same false, hollow smiles that once had looked like nature on *her* face.

Away from all the scandal of the world, and little recking how it hoots and hunts down those who linger on the Course where fresh excitements only quell for one short moment the demand for more, Alick Harley was in utter ignorance of the fact that the reign of her who in his dreams he called the Lady of the Lake was over, and that the stigma of old maidism was beginning to be attached to Miss Louisa Graham.

They met again, when, owing to sundry deaths of unrequited septuagenarians, Alick Harley's chances of a Peerage had raised him infinitely in the world's opinion. He did not see the change that intervening years had wrought upon the features of that world-worn woman—but flattered, gratified, and soothed by her apparent constancy, he fell at once into the snare, and, ere the strange vicissitudes had seemed to have more substance than a dream, the Curate, domiciled at last at Ashington House, and recognized as heir to all its honours, received with blushing front society's congratulations on his great *success!*

The bashful man looked sadly out of his element when, creeping into corners, and away from her who gladly aided him in the retiring process, he hoped to pass unnoticed in the brilliant throng. But earls expectant, however mild their light, must not expect to hide it under bushels; and Alick Harley, finding himself before the lights conspicuously, was forced, however awkwardly, to play his part.

And how they did applaud him! Not aloud—and with broad-clapping palms and shouts of admiration—but with a subtle worship due to wealth, and with the cringing reverence that is rank's reward and punishment. For it was a heavy doom indeed to him, that dragging into public notice. His very legs were burthens to him—the legs that did him such good service in his daily walks amidst his poorest brethren. And then, his arms! Good heavens! to think that human limbs should seem so much *de trop* and cumbersome!

'Why, Harley, my dear fellow, *you* in London! I heard from Susan Brigham you were staying at Cheltenham. They say I must congratulate you on your coming marriage. And so I do—and hope with all my heart you will be happy.'

And Ernest Audaine—for he it was who spoke—shook Alick by the hand again, for he had but small respect for our conventional enactments, and showed his friendly feelings openly when they arose within him.

Alick felt greatly comforted by his old friend's presence, and might have been almost pronounced a happy man, when Ernest, taking him by the arm affectionately, drew him towards an empty room, and began, as in the days gone by, to hold a quiet colloquy away from the din of tongues.

Audaine had a strong motive for thus seeking to engage the Curate in private conversation, for he had to speak to him of Susan—of Susan, who had, after much inward deliberation, consulted him on a matter of vital family importance, and whose own situation—pecuniary and otherwise, was one which loudly called for aid from those interested in her welfare.

But what passed between the Curate and his friend in the small library at Ashington House, must be revealed in another and a shorter chapter.

CHAPTER V.

ALICK HARLEY IS FOUND WANTING.

'It is so hard to catch sight of you now, my dear fellow,' began Audaine, 'that I must not throw away my opportunity. I have called on you no end of times, and almost began to be afraid at last that I must let my pen do duty for my tongue.'

'I have been occupied so much of late,' murmured Alick, who, in truth, felt rather conscience-stricken. 'And if you knew how much I have to do, you would not wonder that even my best friends must sometimes say as you do, that they cannot find me.'

'Oh, do not make apologies,' cried Ernest. 'I know that every station has its duties—and, although you are as yet only standing upon the steps of your exalted throne, you have, of course, to bow before that sovereign thing, the world, till you receive its homage in your turn. Well, it's all right, of course, but still it is a bore for an old friend like me to walk off disappointed daily from the great man's door, and hear the "not-at-home," that means, "I've something pleasanter to do than hear your hum-drum conversation." '

'Hum-drum,' repeated Alick, with a smile, glad, as it seemed, to catch at a chance word to aid in turning off attention from himself. 'Hum-drum. There is mock humility, unworthy of you, Ernest, in the word. Why, dear old fellow, I am behind the scenes at last, and know how greatly valued is my friend's society. Often and often I look back with wonder at myself for never understanding how it was, and not appreciating at its proper rate the privilege I enjoyed in your society.'

'Bosh and humbug,' broke in Ernest, angrily. 'Alick, this is sickening work, and I shall hate society even more than I despise it, if, in this brief space of time, it has taught your honest tongue to flatter. *That*, however, is scarcely a point at issue now, for I have far graver matters to discuss with you than my own humble merits and your noble fortunes.'

'Audaine—this is unkind,' said Alick; 'and I hope that I have not deserved your sarcasms. However, I can only say that I am too happy, and trust I ever shall be, to give my time and best attention to my earliest and most valued friend. And now to business, for by your solemn face I see it is not pleasure that has brought you here to-night.'

They were in a snug, well-lighted room, called by Lord Ashington, and by the household generally, the small library. Not that its walls were lined with books—far from it; but it was a choice retreat, where anyone who wished to read or write might do both comfortably, and with far less of literary *pomp* and *show* than in the grander bookroom of the house. There were two luxuious arm-chairs before the fire, in which the friends ensconced themselves, and Ernest lost no time in responding to Alick's appeal.

'My dear Harley,' he began, 'I know that, situated as you are at present, there is every excuse for your—your—hearing less—I mean, forgetting for the moment some poor friends who, at the present time, are far less happily situated than we are ourselves.'

Alick moved uneasily in his chair as he listened to this home-thrust, for his conscience had but just begun to slumber, and was still easily awakened to a sense of his own shortcomings.

'I know to whom you allude,' he said. 'And I take shame to myself that I have not allowed every consideration to give way to the paramount duty of visiting my excellent cousin and that dear old lady in their affliction, but—'

'My dear Alick,' interrupted Audaine, 'let us leave the past alone, for the present and the future of your cousin and her godmother are looking so black and threatening that we must devote, as far as possible, our thoughts and conversation to them alone. I need not ask you, whether you are willing to make some sacrifice of—what shall I call it, pride? in order to ameliorate the condition, and improve the prospects of the poor prisoner yonder.'

'Indeed, you need not! There is nothing I would not do. Nothing that I would not attempt at least for Susan and for Cousin Chrissy.'

'That is well. And now tell me, can you, when you saw them last?'

The ex-curate—for it is almost needless to say that Alick had abandoned the subordinate duties which were so unsuited to his new dignity—the ex-curate then, looked considerably embarrassed as he attempted a reply to Audaine's question.

'I am afraid I hardly recollect,' he faltered. 'Susan wrote to me last week, and seemed to think it rather tried poor Cousin Chrissy to see many visitors, and so—'

'You do not know how changed your cousin is. How worn and spirit-broken! I can understand the reason why the sight of you should be in some degree repellent to her. Nay, do not look annoyed. I did not mean exactly that; but there is a terrible complication in this case of Cousin Chrissy's, which makes one fear to touch on a wrong string, and so,' he added, with an unsuccessful effort at facetiousness, 'bring the ropes and pulleys about one's ears at once.'

'You had not used to be so cautious,' Alick said, 'and more especially with one you once appeared to think not quite unworthy of your confidence. But now, as we may at any moment be interrupted, tell me in what way you can employ me in this matter, and how that imaginary quality which you call my pride, may be satisfactorily immolated on the altar of friendship.'

Audaine, who had been rather softened

towards his friend by the opening words of his last sentence, felt his heart close once more against the rising man, as the latter wound up his remarks with such sententious roundness. And yet, in thus condemning Alick, as growing rapidly in conceit and 'priggism,' Ernest Audaine was doubtless too severe on one whose want of moral courage was his chief defect. The conduct of the 'weak' through life must, to a great extent, be a mere lottery, and it is not for the strong of purpose, and the uninfluenced (comparatively speaking), by outward causes, to sit in judgment and condemn remorselessly their feebler brethren.

Happily for Alick's peace of mind, the slight symptoms of contempt which Ernest felt for him were not apparent in his old friend's manner, while he said with impressive gravity—

'You do not know, perhaps, that want of money is just now the greatest evil from which our friends are suffering.'

'Is it, indeed? I never thought of that as one among their many trials,' put in Alick.

'Well, then, you know it now,' said Ernest, rather roughly, for he was becoming irritated by the complete, and, as he considered it, the disgraceful ignorance betrayed by Alick, of his cousin's pressing wants and urgent claims on those akin to her for aid and consolation: 'Well, then, you know it now, and I can only wonder that the pecuniary distress of one so excellent and unselfish should not before have occurred to you as probable.'

'I hardly see how it should,' said Alick, who was beginning in his turn to feel rather hurt at the tone which Ernest had assumed. 'I knew that Mrs. Fletcher is rich—very rich she always seemed to me, and how could I suppose that Susan—that her god-daughter should be in want of money at a time like this?'

'Then you have *not* seen her in her wretched one-roomed lodging?' cried Ernest, indignantly. 'You have not been witness to the hourly struggle to hide the penury that is beginning to crush her to the earth? You have not cared to make inquiry as to the disposal of Mrs. Fletcher's riches. You do not know, of course, that suspected persons — I mean those who are to stand a trial for felonious acts—have nothing they can call their own; and therefore that Susan is utterly dependent, even for the means of existence, on such aid as she will accept from others.'

'Poor soul!' said Alick, feelingly; 'I had no idea of this.'

'Of course you had not, for your cousin is not one of those who blazon forth either her virtues or her trials. You should have seen her, Alick, as I did yesterday, to form a proper judgment of Miss Brigham *now*. She was returning from the prison where she had just paid her daily visit—a counted twenty minutes for all the many words those two would gladly say to each other—and I met her walking all alone through the half-melting snow and slippery slush of —— Street, to the wretched lodging where she lives.'

'I can guess now the reason,' remarked Alick, 'why she almost forbade my coming to her. It was because she would not let me see how poor she was. She knew how it would pain me; knew, too, that my own want of means would make it difficult to come, as I most gladly would, to her assistance. Ernest, you look astonished; but the truth is, that the allowance granted so lately to me by Lord Ashington, goes almost entirely to pay off my father's debts, and to enable my mother to live in some degree according to what she calls our new position.'

'Exactly; I had heard that Mrs. Harley had engaged a *bijou* of a house in Bolton Street, and—but no matter—only you are quite wrong, Alick, in your idea that Susan fears your looking on her poverty; and moreover you are not within a hundred miles of guessing why she threw out the hint, which you took (don't be angry) with so much readiness. However, I am forgetting her, poor soul! as I met her yesterday fresh from her errand of mercy, and when she showed me more of her inmost fears and necessities than I had even dreamt of previously. You know there is but little superfluous cash among the Brigham family, and the small help that amongst them they have been able to collect for Susan, is expended by her, partly in extra comforts for her poor old friend, and partly in procuring for herself the means of existence. On the latter circumstance, you, who know her character, can easily understand that Susan Brigham did not care to dwell, but what she *did* enlarge upon, and that with an intensity of feeling which I fully shared, was the absolute necessity of obtaining funds for the legal defence of Mrs. Fletcher in her coming trial. At present there is literally *no* money at her disposal for this purpose; and what is more, unless you, her near relation, can do something for her assistance, I see no chance of her obtaining any.'

'But what can I do in this emergency?' asked Alick. 'Ah, if Clayton were but here! I have written to him by this Packet, and if

I had only known the great need that there is for money, I would have asked him to give to Cousin Chrissy of his abundance.'

'An omission which I have been fortunate enough to remedy,' said Audaine, gravely; 'and believe me that on no one does the duty of defending Mrs. Fletcher fall more decidedly than on Clayton Bernard. But, in the meantime, and as many weeks must elapse before an answer can arrive from Clayton, something must be done at once in furtherance of the object we have in view; and, Alick, since the honour—I mean, since the happiness—of some of your connections is involved in this miserable business, I think you might appeal to Lord Ashington both for advice and pecuniary assistance for your cousin and her godmother.'

Audaine looked full at Alick Harley as he made this startling proposition, and was nothing surprised to see that, notwithstanding the melancholy picture he had drawn of Susan's distress, Alick did not seem particularly charmed by the means pointed out to him for its removal.

'I would do anything in my power,' he said, hesitatingly, 'but I fear Lord Ashington would think it rather a liberty—I mean rather strange—on my part, were I to ask him for assistance in the case of a—no! she is not even a relation of my own—I mean poor Mrs. Fletcher; and I do not see on what plea I could apply to my cousin for charitable aid in this instance.'

'Charitable aid! Good Heavens, Alick, if you did but know what I know—if you could but for an instant dream—But I have promised, at least for the present, conditional secresy. Should, however, one event occur, which is, I greatly fear, only too probable, why then you will understand my motive for applying to you, and through you to a man who may be deeply interested in this coming trial.'

'You speak in riddles; nor can I see at present how, except that Susan Brigham is my near relation, her pecuniary distress should interest Lord Ashington more than that of any other poor, unhappy creature whose wants are greater than her means.'

'You cannot? Well, I trust the day will never come when you will understand more clearly how that, for interested and selfish motives alone, you would do well to move a *little* for your old friend's good. More, far more, turns on Mrs. Fletcher's acquittal than you at present know of; but the time *may* come—God grant it should not—when you will cease to wonder at the perseverance with which I have urged this duty on you. I am a poor man now myself, as you well know; and, indeed, were I a millionaire, I greatly doubt if Susan Brigham would consent to be my debtor. But, needy though I am, I may yet be able to exert some influence for our poor old friend, and to-morrow will endeavour to see ——,' and he mentioned the name of a distinguished barrister, 'who, when he knows all the circumstances, may be induced to undertake the case.'

'How fortunate you are,' said Alick, 'to possess both the power and the will to do good!' And then, seeing that Ernest was making a move, preparatory, as it appeared, to his departure, he added, deprecatingly, 'Audaine, I fear you think me lukewarm in this matter. I fear that—'

'Of course I do; and what is more, I suspect that you are beginning to lose in this great house, and amongst your new connections, the honest independence both of will and character that sat so well upon you in your less prosperous days. I have no right to speak in this way, I dare say, but we are long-tried friends, and, as I said before, but for a solemn promise, I could give you ample reasons for my seeming importunity. So now, good night, old fellow; go back to your pleasant company, and to your bride elect, forgetting, if you can, the poor, weak, mourning cousin trudging through the snow—and Cousin Chrissy, in a felon's cell, eating of prison fare, and drinking the bitter cup which you might help to sweeten if you would.'

He was gone before Alick—who had been greatly startled by the energy with which his friend had pronounced the concluding words—had in any degree recovered from the effect they had produced. He was very much distressed by the conflicting feelings which the preceding conversation had conjured up within him, and was far from feeling inclined to follow Ernest's advice, and return to the 'goodly companie' which he had quitted a short half-hour before with such widely different feelings. There was nothing now remaining in his breast of that agreeable consciousness of being at last in his right place, which had made him almost forget his constitutional shyness, while listening to the *empressés* greetings of his many new acquaintances. He had been hearing *truth* in the short interval that had elapsed since he had left that brilliantly-lighted and well-thronged assembly-room, and now, shrinking within himself, and half fearing to face the whispered reproaches of his tardily-awakened conscience, Alick Harley remained, even as Audaine had left him, ensconced within the shelter of his easy chair, and notwithstanding the brilliant future which awaited him, an anything but enviable man.

The real truth was, although the fact was not guessed at by himself, that Alick Harley felt thoroughly ashamed of his conduct. He knew—none better, would he have but been honest with himself—how entirely despicable was the motive for his unwillingness to mention Susan to his noble relation; for, in common with many who have lived out of the pale of the best society, he entertained a vague idea that the contempt felt by 'small' people for the trading classes is often shared by the so-called 'great;' and therefore any mention of his cousin, which might involve an explanatory notice of her birth and parentage, was eminently distasteful to him.

Alick was, as yet, far from feeling either at

home or at his ease with the 'fine people' amongst whom he had been so suddenly transplanted. It was singular, but nevertheless unhappily true, that he who had seemed to stand so firm when the waves of poverty and adversity dashed against the rock on which he stood, had drifted away, even as a rudderless vessel upon a shoreless sea, when the enervating breath of prosperity filled the silken sails, and bore him far away from his safe anchorage.

It may seem to many (who, imagining that their own standing is secure, are also probably in danger of falling), that Alick Harley's weakness is overdrawn, and that he has yielded prematurely to temptation. To this objection I can only reply, that this feeble Christian had never been in the smallest degree prepared for the great change which had come upon him, and that, therefore, he was at first like one bewildered and confused. Sin too—the kind of sin to which he was yielding—did not appear to him in the startling form of evidently broken commandments, or in that of any of the coarser vices from which his better nature would have shrunk instinctively; but the progress of evil within him was not the less sure because it was insidious; and that this was the case had become in some degree apparent to himself, during his brief colloquy with the outspoken and uncompromising Ernest Audaine.

During the course of the unpleasant self examination which followed on his Mentor's departure, Alick resolved not only to be more watchful over himself, his motives, and his conduct, but also he made a sort of mental promise that he would endeavour to 'do something' for those whose cause had just been so urgently pleaded before him. He did not as yet go quite the length of resolving that he would at once make known their wants to the cousin, a small portion of whose superfluities would have been so well employed in providing for those that were in need; but still he would exert himself in some way, and regain, if possible, the ground he had evidently lost in Ernest Audaine's opinion.

It was a very vague plan of a campaign that which Alick Harley thus hastily sketched, and it showed how imperfect was his estimate of the forces which would be brought in array against him. Moreover, his own exceeding moral weakness was a disadvantage on his own side which he had failed to take into account, for he was in utter ignorance of the fact that he stood in positive awe of almost every inmate of Ashington House.

From the aged Earl, whose gouty fingers he feared to press too familiarly, to the groom-of-the-chambers, who seemed so infinitely more at home and at his ease in those lofty apartments than he did himself—towards each and all he felt a vague but overweening respect, which tended greatly to diminish the daily comfort of his existence.

In short, Alick Harley, melancholy as is the admission, was, as I have before hinted, beginning to serve two masters, and already the galling yoke of his new slavery was making itself felt in the loss not only of his own peace of conscience, but in the threatened contempt of those whose good opinion he could not choose but value.

CHAPTER VI.

LADY ANNABELLA'S LECTURE ON BEHAVIOUR.

'WHAT an immense relief it will be to get out of London!' was the remark one morning of Miss Louisa's worldly mamma. 'Only fancy—London at Christmas! I haven't done such a thing since I can remember as find myself in Curzon Street in December.'

'You never had so good a reason before,' sneered Sir Carlton Graham, Lady Annabella's husband, in answer to the above speech. 'It isn't every day one catches such a fine young fellow as the Curate for one's daughter—especially when one's daughter has hung on hand a little. How many seasons is it—eh, Louisa—since you shone out before the world as a grown-up young lady?

Not twenty is it, quite? Well, something very like it. But never mind, I'll bet the Curate won't inquire into such trifling matters; and he prefers his Bible to Debrett, of course.'

Miss Louisa Graham, the bride elect of Alick Harley, had been too well accustomed to these and similar speeches from her not over-delicate-minded father, to show any symptoms of emotion on the present occasion. She was seated close to one of the three windows which gave light to the spacious front drawing-room of the Graham's London house, and was pursuing the identical employment, in the identical place which, season after season, for the better part of a quarter of a century, had been the scene of her maidenly morning avocations.

How very tired the poor lady had grown of the wearisome routine of her existence none knew better than herself; but none succeeded better in concealing from the world the every-day disgust she was enduring.

She had some friends who saw the deepening lines upon her forehead, and did not scruple to assert that to poor dear Louisa's lessening chances of a settlement might be attributed the careworn, haggard look she often wore.

'There is her sister now,' said a middle-aged and very experienced lady—one of those iron-duchesses, veterans in the world's campaigns, who could, 'an if they would,' relate some chronicles at which society might well grow pale—'There is her sister, now, that kind, obliging Mrs. Jephson. She is older than poor Loo by a year or two, and see how well she wears. It is all because she's settled. To be sure, her husband must have been taken as a mere *pis aller*—a man with such a name!—who bought with a few thousand pounds a year the fancied right to call her great connections *his* relations. But what did Laura care? He was a husband, after all, and she can now set old Sir Carleton and his temper at defiance.'

There was much truth in this opinion of the duchess's, for the enduring of the domestic tyrant's temper was certainly one cause of the too-early crowsfeet which had begun to show themselves on Louisa's peevish face. But it is time to return to the conversation which this slight family sketch has interrupted.

Lady Annabella was writing notes with a golden pen, at a table where every ornament, and, indeed, where every writing utensil seemed to be formed out of the precious metal; for she was a woman greatly addicted to parade and show. She liked to queen it over humble people—to dazzle and distress them by her wealth and grandeur—after which charitable operation she was wont to look superciliously down upon her victims with an insolence which must have been highly satisfactory to her own self-importance and inherent love of power.

They were a thoroughly well-assorted couple, those two cold and selfish world-worshippers, who had grown gray in the hard service which they had vowed to Mammon. They had been badly paid in some respects for the fierce battle they had fought in the close ranks of their exacting master; and why, and for what adequate motive they had spent the best years of their lives in doing mercenaries' service, it seemed hard to say, for their income was one which placed them in the category of the rich; and they had no sons—only three comparatively inexpensive daughters to provide for. Of these, two were still unmarried, but the eldest, who had been intended by nature for a plain (very plain, as some asserted) country girl, with honest, simple tastes, had, after being drilled into a 'fine' but rather spurious kind of lady, married a wealthy *parvenu*; whilst the still plainer Janet yet remained on hand, as well as Miss Louisa, who having been beguiled by an early promise of rich beauty, had waxed proud and difficult of choice, and was now suffering for her folly under the infliction of incipient old-maidism.

The possession of these two candidates for matrimony had not tended either to improve the tempers or increase the popularity of the Grahams, whose persevering 'finery' and insolence—the relics of a bygone generation's efforts at exclusiveness—had long made them the laughing-stock of a world which no longer tolerates when it ceases to be entertained.

It chanced that on that particular morning, Lady Annabella, who was, as I have said, one of a former school in coarseness of manner and open impertinence of demeanour and of speech,—Lady Annabella, then, although a duke's daughter and a lady of high degree, was, on that especial morning in an irritable state of mind, which was aggravated by the sound of Mr. Graham's creaking boots, as they, or rather their owner, walked with a horrid regularity of step up and down the room. He had a habit of stopping, too, from time to time, and at apparently stated intervals, behind his wife's chair; on which occasions he would say interrogatively, and with an evident desire for a reply,—

'Well, Lady Annabella?' to which interesting and impressive query the lady would respond, without so much as raising her head from her employment—

'Well, Mr. Graham;' and then the promenade would continue again as systematically as before.

Even in the days of her youth Louisa had found herself sometimes wondering whether the father and mother—whom in the fifth commandment she was so decidedly called upon to honour—had in reality any claim to that distinction. She had no recollection of any pleasant instances, either of parental tenderness towards herself, or of conjugal yielding towards one another. Moreover, it had not seemed to her that from either of them she had ever received any particular lessons, either of religion or morality, to guide her through her future life; and this being the case, Miss Louisa was perhaps justified in limiting her obedience to the rule of life to a merely mechanical yielding to the second clause in the commandment.

Lady Annabella was one of those family-women who object especially to a passive endurance of the ills of existence; nor was silence under aggravation a quality held by her in the slightest degree of estimation. She looked up, therefore, from under her heavy eyebrows with much severity at her silent daughter, and, in default of other means of rousing her to wrath, said, spitefully—

'Pray, when do you intend to commence the education of your rustic admirer, my dear Louisa? Soon, I hope, for there really is no time to lose. What with the vast amount he has to learn, and what to unlearn, you will find you have enough to do, I suspect, in licking him into shape.'

It was not a pretty form of speech, the one chosen by Lady Annabella, and Louisa would have felt intense satisfaction in explaining to her mamma that education in manners, in that particular house, should begin with the higher powers; but true to the rule she had laid down for herself, she resisted the temptation, and kept silence even from good words.

'We shall be having your friend exposing his ignorance of the world and good society at Richmond,' continued Lady Annabella. 'For my part, I cannot understand his caring to come among people with whose very language he is unacquainted, and where he is certain to make some awkward *bévue* by touching on subjects of which he knows nothing.'

'There you are wrong,' said Sir Carleton, with his usual self-satisfied sneer, and stopping for a moment in his walk; 'there you are quite wrong, for I do not know anyone with whom subjects in general are more safe from profane handling than with our friend Alick. His talent for silence is fully developed, and I hardly think that any lessons of Louisa's will improve him.'

'Practice makes perfect,' said Lady Annabella, with another meaning glance at her daughter.

'And example is better than precept,' added Sir Carleton, stopping this time opposite to Louisa, whose temper was, to his infinite satisfaction, beginning to show symptoms of a coming explosion. 'Not much chance of a quarrel between you and the Curate if you both determine to hold your tongues. 'Gad! how I do hate a sulky disposition. I'd rather hear a woman break out, as you do sometimes, my lady, than see her shut up her humours till they grow so d—d acrid that they poison all the blood in her veins. I'd rather see her—'

But at this moment the family bickering was brought to an abrupt halt by the sudden announcement of a visitor, in the shape of a no less important personage than the bridegroom elect.

It will be readily believed that the house in Curzon Street, where that amiable family abided, was not one in which a shy and by no means self-assured young suitor was likely to find his position an agreeable one. There are some families in the world where consanguineous jealousies and hatreds either slumber or do not exist—families where a pleasant familiarity and a mutual confidence reign throughout the house, and where the affianced lover is greeted with beaming smiles, which make him glide at once and easily into the groove prepared for him.

But for Alick, the unfashioned and all unworld-taught man — whose coronet in prospect could but barely make amends for what Lady Annabella called his shabby figure, his unmitigated *gaucherie*, and his unfathomable ignorance in the wisdom of the world—for *him*, for that poor bashful lover, there was no cordial welcome, and no reassuring words to bid him go on and prosper.

To see Alick Harley, in a costume which always looked like his 'Sunday's best,' enter the drawing-room, no one would imagine that he was so soon to become united by the closest ties to that extremely undemonstrative family. He brought his hat with him in his hand, and sat down with it between his knees, as though ready on the slightest hint to make his parting bow, and leave that most ungenial presence for the society of humbler friends, and of acquaintances less exacting in the matter of appearances.

'How d'ye do, Mr. Harley?' said Lady Annabella, holding out one stiff and well-gloved finger towards him, after a fashion which the visitor could scarcely fail to see was intended to be repellent. 'How d'ye do? There—keep at arms' length till you can tell me that you have not been among those horrid fevers again. They're always taken about in wool, and you don't smoke, I believe?'

'Indeed I don't, Lady Annabella. Nothing would induce me,' stammered poor Alick, 'to come into a lady's room after smoking a cigar. But I really never have smoked since I was at college. I could hardly afford it then, and afterwards, when I was a curate—'

'You had of course to spend all your money in mutton chops and tallow candles. But take my advice, and smoke now, as every one else does—you will only make yourself absurd by being different from other people, and if you will go among putrid fevers you run less chance of bringing them back to us poor people who are not so piously inclined.'

There was a pause in the conversation after this sally of Lady Annabella's—a pause which Alick took advantage of by creeping closer to Louisa's embroidery frame, and whispering a few affectionate words over the canvas. She looked up at him with the nearest approach to genuine pleasure that had ever yet lighted up her face when Alick had addressed her, and he, feeling in his heart the warm reflection of that unusual glow, came nearer still, and was half meditating on the possibility of using words of softer meaning, when Lady Annabella's high-pitched voice sent scattering to the winds the light-winged thoughts.

'Are you thinking of going to Richmond, Mr. Harley?' she said; 'you would think it a tremendous party, I dare say, and very likely would be happier at home. There's Lady A——, who is supposed to be awfully crushing, and the Duchess of B——, who walks over everybody. However, of course you will please yourself.'

Louisa looked with some wistful anxiety at her lover during her mother's speech—and he, poor man, being still under the influence of her fleeting smile of welcome, was happy enough to attribute her glance of inquiry to an unspoken desire for his presence at Lord Ashington's Richmond villa. A moment before, he had been congratulating himself on the good fortune which enabled him to plead a prior engagement in excuse for declining to accept his relation's invitation; but now—so little versed was he in the human face divine—he regretted that he would be forced to disappoint the expectations of his betrothed, and was already casting about for a means of eluding his former promise.

'I am very sorry,' he began. 'But several weeks ago I promised to spend next Saturday till Monday with the Claverings at Craven Bank, and I hardly see how I can disappoint them now.'

'The Claverings,' said Sir Carleton, musingly. 'Is that the man who makes his money no one knows how, and who has a house in Grosvenor Place, and a wife that Ernest Audaine makes love to?'

The description was too correct in some respects for Alick to plead ignorance of its truth, but, with all his awe of his future father-in-law, he ventured to demur against the latter clause.

'You have been strangely misinformed, sir,' he said, 'if you have been told that any one, least of all my friend Mr. Audaine, has ever—has at any time forgot himself so far as to—,' but here, poor Alick, who was deplorably ill 'up' in such synonyms as are in use for the portraying of the fashionable vice to which Sir Carleton had alluded, finding himself totally at a loss for a correct expression, prudently held his peace.

Sir Carleton laughed—that hollow, wounding, conventional laugh which strikes so chill to the heart of earnest people; but it was too much trouble to attempt the initiation of his son-in-law into the A B C of the great world's mysteries; and besides, the hour was come for him to stare (even as he had done any time these forty years) out of the Club's bay-window, with his great gold eye-glass in his eye, and his auburn curls, which deceived nobody, falling gracefully over the crowsfeet which encircled his keen gray eyes.

Lady Annabella continued, after his departure, to make invidious remarks on the Claverings generally, and on Marian in particular, concluding her sarcasms by saying, with more than usual acerbity of manner, 'You will find, Mr. Harley, that if you hope to live in our world, you must shake off those sort of people. You won't find it very easy, I dare say, for they're awfully pushing generally, I believe. How long have you known these Scavengings —I beg your pardon—what did you say their name was?'

'Clavering,' answered Alick, plucking up all his courage, and, indeed, he had grown something bolder since the reduction of the enemies' forces caused by the departure of Sir Carleton. 'Clavering is the name of my friends, and indeed, I may say my connections, for Mrs. Clavering is the sister of Clayton Bernard, who so lately married my sister.'

'Oh, indeed! and he was a man of some property, was he not? And do tell me about your sister—one never met her hardly in good places. She was rather horsy, wasn't she? Fast, you know—and men talked about her, didn't they?'

'Oh, mamma!' remonstrated Louisa, who

notwithstanding her experience of the Curate's powers of endurance, began to be seriously alarmed at the possible consequence of this mental torture. 'Oh, mamma—you must be thinking of some one else—you always confuse people's names, and you know that only so lately as Lady P——'s large party, Mr. Audaine was talking to you about Mrs. Clayton Bernard, and praising her and her husband beyond everything.'

'Oh, he is paid, of course, for that sort of thing,' said Lady Annabella, laughing coarsely. 'Ernest Audaine is bound in honour to stand up for the morals of every one connected with Mrs. Clavering, if all the stories one hears are true. But now, perhaps, you will be so good as to inform me whether you are going with me to Garrard's about that brooch to-day. It is an odious swop, and Lord Ashington is very mean, in my opinion, not to let you have the family jewels new set at once.'

Alick had listened to this, to him scarcely

incomprehensible conversation, till his brain was almost dizzy with the confusing images it called up before him. In the first place, there was a stain thrown on the white robe of that dove-eyed Marian Clavering, whose virtue had been to him before a thing as unquestionable as Gospel truth. And next came Ernest, with his high, chivalrous sense of honour—a blasted being now—for if that crafty Lady Annabella spoke the truth, he was false to his friend, to his principles, and to his God!

But such, and harrowing as were these, to him, novel ideas, they were as every-day pleasantries compared to the possibility of there being any foundation for the hints thrown out by that inhuman lady against his sister Florence. It was true that Alick had only the most confused notions of his future mother-in-law's meaning, when she touched on the subject of poor Flo's delinquencies; but there was a contemptuous *persiflage* in her tone which was apparent even to him, and which filled him with a vague alarm for the honour of his family. Then, too, came the puzzling allusions to the Ashington jewels, with the wish, which he could only trust was not shared by his betrothed, that the decease of the old nobleman should be forestalled by the appropriation of the splendid diamonds now reposing peacefully in their caskets. All these things were distressing in the extreme to the unfortunate Alick, and the more so from the entanglement into which this new view of life had plunged his hitherto simple ideas. For some time he remained floating in a sea of doubt and difficulty, and was only roused by hearing Louisa whisper, with as much plaintive sweetness as she could master for the occasion,—

'Never mind mamma, dear Mr. Harley, she is so odd, you know; and of course go to your friends' (Loo was dreadfully afraid that he would change his mind); 'I shall miss you terribly, but you will think of me sometimes.' And with her head bent towards him tenderly, she acted the pleading 'sweetheart' to perfection.

Another look, and Alick would probably —for he was human after all, and Louisa Graham was still a 'fine woman,'—have so far vanquished his natural timidity as to go through some of the forms (seeing that Lady Annabella had left them to their *tête-à-tête*) which are customary among engaged lovers. But Loo saw the danger in time, and skilfully avoided it by a hasty allusion to her proposed drive.

'I am so sorry to go,' she said, 'but you know that mamma must be kept in good humour, and I shall see you soon again—on Wednesday, will it not be? And oh, by-the-by, will Mr. Audaine be at Craven Bank? He is so horridly satirical, and says such spiteful things.'

'Does he? I never heard him. He has always been so kind to me—I cannot fancy Ernest could ever be ill-natured.'

'Well, perhaps I am wrong; but I

have heard he is not always to be trusted about people's age, you know, and that kind of thing. You understand what I mean?'

'Indeed I don't, but I could ask him; I mean I could set anything right with Ernest that you wished him to know.'

'Oh, please don't say a word to him of my remarks,' said Miss Louisa, with some pettishness, which, however, she did her best to conceal. 'You need not say a word to him of me. And, Alick' (here her voice grew tender again), 'be sure you do not stay there after Wednesday; I shall suspect you of an admiration for the pretty cousin if you do.'

Alick was unmeasurably gratified by this most unexpected proof of affection. To inspire the feeling of love was indeed as new as it was gratifying; but when the delightful truth became apparent that this queenly woman, this peerless ruler of fashion, was actually jealous of *him*, the humble curate, the rustic on whom the smiles of beauty had never yet been lavished, then he felt at last that he had not lived in vain, and that an earthly heaven was opening out upon his sight.

CHAPTER VII.

MR. CLAVERING RECEIVES A TELEGRAM.

THERE are some heads of families whose return to their home after a more than usually lengthened absence is decidedly not a signal for rejoicing. We have all heard of such unamiable specimens of the class *paterfamilias*, and some of us, no doubt, have been unfortunately able from our own observation to bear testimony to the truth of my remark. A gradual gloom and an increasing stillness pervades the family and household as the hour approaches when the presence of the master of the house may be expected; and the servants, who, in their hours of comparative liberty, have grown lax in the performance of their daily duties, hasten to cast a veneering covering over the glaring evidences of their negligence; whilst the very children, even to the youngest-born, aware that their time of joyous freedom is at an end, grow dull and solemn, speaking beneath their breath, and treading 'delicately,' as if in fear of punishment and anger.

There was an almost ominous silence about Craven Bank when Marian's carriage, bearing its graceful occupant, stopped at the lodge-gate, through which the Station 'fly' had just one hour previously drawn Mr. Leo Clavering, with all his travelling property.

That gentleman's indignation was great, and only exceeded by his surprise, when he found that Mrs. Clavering was not at home to felicitate him and herself on his return.

'Gone to London!' he exclaimed, with an expletive which is better left unrepeated. 'Gone to London! and since when?'

'Only since the morning, sir,' replied Mrs. Dawson, to whom the question was addressed. 'Mrs. Clavering didn't take no servant up to London with her; the carriage was told to meet her at the other Station.'

'Hang it—that's cool,' muttered Clavering to himself; 'she must have known that I was coming, too, and should require the carriage. I say, did your mistress mention that I was expected home this afternoon?'

'Mrs. Clavering didn't say nothink to me,' responded the lady's-maid. 'It's possible that she did just mention it to John, or to the housekeeper in ordering dinner.'

'Go to the devil,' said Clavering in a rage, 'and tell the coachman on your way he needn't take the carriage out to-night. I'll teach her,' he continued to himself, 'to order out my domestics and my horses, in all this frost and snow too, and letting me come home in a d—d fly, that smelt of mouldy stable-boys and stale tobacco.'

As may be supposed, the meeting between Marian and her indignant spouse was not remarkable for any signal display of conjugal affection; and it was, perhaps, just as well for the preservation in the establishment of Mr. Clavering's tottering character as a gentleman, that his loud, overbearing tones whilst addressing his rebellious wife, were reduced to comparative silence by the timely arrival of guests.

The dinner that day at Craven Bank was rendered considerably more agreeable to Marian by the presence of Ernest Audaine, who, with Alick Harley, had been asked to spend a few days at the villa. To Alick (whose habits were retiring, and who, as I have endeavoured to render apparent, was easily quelled by either real or fancied superiority arrogated by those with whom he lived) a visit to his purse-proud host would have been unendurable save for the protecting presence of his friend Audaine. But with Ernest as his guest the speculator became a different man, for the quiet, unfamiliar, high-bred bearing of one who stood so high in the great world's opinion, awed the man of money into a temporary forgetfulness of his own importance, and kept his irritable temper under salutary control.

That something more than usual had occurred to rouse the demon of wrath in Clavering's breast was evident to both Ernest and his friend the moment that, with a lowering brow, and a manner constrained till it was almost uncourteous, he advanced to meet them. The early part of the dinner passed away unpleasantly enough, for Marian found it impossible to shake off the fear she felt of the frowning eyes before her, and the attempts at anything like conversation which were made by Ernest Audaine meeting with no encouragement, an awkward silence soon threatened to prevail amongst the party. Ernest endeavoured to keep his eyes from dwelling upon Marian's pallid face and quivering lips; whilst she, contrasting the hard, coarse, angry countenance before her with the intellectual brow and silent, sympathizing glance of him whose every thought was hers, hugged to her beating heart that dangerous comfort, the while she schooled her speaking face to show no signs of feeling.

After awhile, however, (for it is rare indeed that a free indulgence in 'generous' wine fails to produce some effect in opening the mouth for other purposes besides that of ministering to the body's wants), after awhile, then, and towards the close of that gloomy repast, Clavering's tongue was loosened, and he began to speak; not pleasantly, however, or even with an effort to make amends for his previous unhost-like taciturnity, but with the pugnacious argumentativeness which with him always terminated in bluster, and with the obtrusive advice to every one on every subject, which was neither more nor less than bullying.

Marian soon escaped from this, to her, unpleasant scene; but Clavering, greatly to the annoyance of his guests, continued his libations to a late hour, whilst with every glass he drank he grew less seemly in his talk, and his accustomed boasts of wealth and greatness increased in their audacity. Audaine was growing infinitely wearied and disgusted with his host's insufferable self-importance, and he was planning an ingenious mode of escape from its infliction, when his attention, which had more than begun to wander, was arrested by the sound of a name which both he and Harley had sufficiently painful causes for remembering.

'It was a deuce of a bore, you know,' Clavering was saying, 'travelling, as of course I did, through France and Belgium with what they call a suite—though there was no one but my groom and valet. It is a deuced bore though, really, the way they put things in the papers. They said that I was travelling with Milor Annesley. Now Milor Annesley may be thought a very good fellow amongst the Dooks, but I've a character to keep up, and didn't choose to put up with such an imputation.'

'It does not require any great amount either of fastidiousness or high-mindedness,' remarked Andaine, 'to decline the society of a man who lies under the imputation of having committed a forgery; but where did you fall in with Annesley? I fancied he was in America; he is making a mistake, I suspect, in showing himself.'

'Of course he is. And what the devil he was about at Lille is more than I can tell you; but there he was. And there, there happened just two nights ago the very rummest thing! You know the hotel at Lille? A great, old shambling place, with doors that rattle on their hinges, and where you are more uncomfortable than in any other house on the Continent.'

'I never stopped there,' said Audaine, feeling that he was expected to make some response to his host's observations.

'No more would anyone in their senses; but, somehow, on Thursday night I felt so very little inclined to take the rail again for Dover at two a.m., that I resolved to stop the night at Lille. I saw that black sheep Annesley in the *Buffet*, and endeavoured to avoid him' (which was not the fact); 'but you know that men who are under a cloud, and that kind of thing, won't let you pass them by—they try to hang on to your respectability. Well, as I couldn't shake him off, I thought I'd make the best of it; and as I'd nothing else to do, we sat and smoked till twelve o'clock had struck.'

'I dare say it was a very jolly time you spent,' said Ernest; 'for Annesley was a pleasant fellow once, and might have been a worthy member of society if he had not had a duke for his father, and five hundred a-year for his *ménus plaisirs.*'

'I don't see the harm of five hundred a-year—except that it sings deuced small to fifty thousand; but that has nothing to do with the h— of a row that Annesley got into that night. I tell you the story as the poor devil told it to me, when I saw him with his head bound up next morning. It seems they put him in a bed-room, which was only separated from another by what I believe is called a *cloison,* and that the two great folding-doors, ill-fitting and scarcely fastened, allowed of every whisper in the adjoining apartment being heard distinctly. Well, according to his own account, Annesley tumbled into bed at once, and went to sleep directly, which was highly probable, seeing that he had imbibed some dozen glasses of cognac at my expense; but he wasn't allowed to sleep in peace in that confounded place, for towards the small hours he was awoke by screams which he, and indeed the whole house, declared were the most loud and awful ever uttered. At first, poor Annesley thought the screamer had made good her entrance (for it was a woman's voice) into his sleeping-chamber; but, as on listening attentively he heard the door being fiercely shaken on the other side, he perceived to his relief that he was mistaken. Still, however, there was small consolation in the slight rampart of defence, for at every moment he expected to see the canvas-and-paper door fly open, and the lunatic—which, judging from her strange, unnatural cries, she certainly was—rush madly to attack him.'

'How very unpleasant,' suggested Alick, whose nerves were none of the strongest, and who was becoming worked up to a high pitch of interest in Clavering's story.

'Very, indeed,' continued the narrator. 'And the more so, as Annesley and the maniac had been stowed away in a distant corner of the overgrown building where bells failed to perform their office, and where assistance, in case of any emergency, would be necessarily long in coming. It seems that Annesley was strongly impressed with this idea, for notwithstanding his extremely light attire (he having sprung out of bed to defend himself) and the coldness of the night, he hung on like grim death, till by degrees the efforts to burst open the door on the other side relaxed, the unearthly howls gradually ceased, and Annesley, feeling at last that he might do so with safety, returned to his bed, and slept soundly.'

'And was that all?' inquired Audaine, who was beginning to condemn the adventure as scarcely worth listening to.

'By no means; for the best, or rather the worst for Annesley, is yet to come—although I can tell you nothing from his own authority of what that something was. My informant, as regards the second act of the drama, is no larger a personage than the Boots of the hotel, who obeying the orders he had received to call Annesley at six o'clock, knocked at his door at the hour appointed. He thundered loudly, as those brutes always do, but receiving no answer, he took the liberty of walking in to see if *milord* was *souffrant*, and required any assistance in his power to render. "*Ah, mossieu*," said the poor Boots, whose hair still stood on end with horror as he described to me what he had seen—"*Ah, mossieu, mais c était affreux! Figurez-vous—ce pauvre Monsieur sur le lit—du sang partout, et une jeune dame, ou demoiselle—ma foi, je n'en sais rien, qui était en train de lui abîmer le front avec un chandelier.*"'

'And this was really true? How shocking!' exclaimed Ernest. 'And what happened next? Annesley was alive, of course, or we should have heard of his death?'

'Alive!—I believe you. It takes more than a woman's blow with a flat-candlestick to knock the life out of a fellow like old George. But I suspect his nerves were out of order—he seemed confounded shaky; and then the *garçon* seemed to think the girl—she was a lunatic escaped from a *maison de santé* at Bruxelles—had been an old acquaintance, for as the doctors, of whom two were sent for, took her from the room, she called out twice the name of "George," and then fell back insensible.'

On hearing the sequel of this singular story, Alick and Audaine's eyes met with a much-meaning expression in their serious faces, and Ernest, who in common with his friend felt more than half convinced that the name of that unhappy lady was not unknown to him, was about to address some more questions to Clavering on the subject, when the entrance of the butler arrested his words.

'A telegraphic message, sir,' said the man, as he handed the salver on which lay the startling missive to his master; 'and the bearer says you'll be so good as sign.'

Instead of complying with this necessary form, Clavering, from whose face every vestige of colour had vanished, started up with an oath, and desired that his carriage might be got ready immediately.

'A summons to town on urgent business,' he said, the moment he was able to speak in any degree collectedly; 'but I shall be back in good time to-morrow, so you must make yourselves at home. No, pray don't go,' he added, forestalling Ernest's attempt at refusal—'I quite expect to find you here on my return.' And so saying, and without waiting for a reply, Clavering hurried from the room, and five minutes later the wheels of his chariot were heard grinding along the gravel road, from which a rapid thaw had already melted away the thickly-fallen snow.

CHAPTER VIII.

AUDAINE SPEAKS HIS MIND ABOUT HIS HOST.

When the two guests, in a state of considerable surprise at the sudden summons which had deprived them of their host's agreeable society, returned to the drawing-room, they found it empty; for Marian had long since retired to her own apartment, there to indulge, without fear of interruption, in the perilous luxury of reverie.

After a single rapid glance round the tenantless apartment, Ernest threw himself into an easy chair (Marian's accustomed seat), and Alick, following the example set him by his companion, made himself comfortable for the remaining portion of the evening.

'I see,' began Audaine, when the coffee and the *chasse* had been discussed, and they were left alone to their conjectures,—'I see that your surmises, or rather your conclusions, are the same as mine, and that you are in no doubt of the fact that the unhappy, crazy girl at Lille, and poor Margaret Mayford are identical.'

'There certainly seems every probability of its being so,' rejoined Harley; 'but what a singular coincidence—what an awful retribution rather, that she should meet with her worst enemy in that unexpected manner, and should avenge herself so terribly with her own weak hands.'

'It is the first time,' mused Ernest, 'since the imprisonment of poor Mrs. Fletcher that I have ceased to lament it; for now we may succeed in keeping this terrible story from her. Only imagine what she would feel, poor soul, were she to hear that that unhappy girl, whose insanity—as Cousin Chrissy hoped—was always harmless, had escaped from her confinement, and commenced a murderous attack upon the author of all her misery!'

'I should be very sorry, also,' suggested

Alick, 'were any rumour of the kind to add to Susan's cares. She felt for Margaret Mayford as a sister, and this news would be a crushing blow to her.'

There was silence between them for awhile, a silence which was broken by Ernest's saying, as though answering to his own thoughts—

'How every phase and portion of this great calamity which has fallen on Mrs. Fletcher's house is to be attributed to men's selfish profligacy and to women's inherent weakness. It was weakness, and the abject fear of saying "No" to a specious, scheming villain that brought about poor Cousin Chrissy's ill-fated union, and entailed, by breaking off poor Margaret's marriage, this fearful visitation on the poor child's head.'

'But from what a dreadful alternative she escaped!' said Alick; 'for what a life must hers have been had she married Lord George Annesley! A man without principle, without religion, and without heart!'

'There you are wrong; for not only is Annesley not that faulty monster which the world ne'er saw, namely, a man born into the world without the possession on which you set such value, but he had besides the good or evil fortune to retain that possession longer than most men who are reared in the lap of luxury, and doomed to a life of idleness.'

Harley was too much in the habit of submitting his own opinion with a blind obedience to that of his older friend, to dispute with him on the fitness of Lord George Annesley to make a woman's married life a happy one. Perhaps, too, there were certain tender memories connected with the deserted girl which crowded round him now, and made him view with scanty charity the conduct of her betrayer.'

'Yes, it is quite true,' continued Ernest, 'that ten years ago George Annesley gave good promise of a better future than the one we must deplore. It was just ten years ago when the poor boy got into his first gambling difficulty, and that did all the mischief. It is a melancholy consideration—and one which those set in authority over us seem never sufficiently to consider—how much depends on the first friendship a lad may form—often, too, on the first woman whom he may love; whilst in nine cases out of ten his ultimate career in life is influenced by some miserable consideration of money, which by lowering his moral tone, and by placing him in a degrading position, eventually works his ruin.'

Ernest rose as he spoke, and holding out his hand, wished his friend 'Good night,' for, as he remarked, it was his intention to leave Craven Bank before breakfast.

'Without saying a word to Mrs. Clavering!' exclaimed Alick, in surprise. 'Remember, her husband urged us to remain, and—'

'Alick!' interrupted Audaine, reseating himself, 'I have lost all patience with that man—that brute I should rather call him—and, but that I see a crisis coming, in which my presence may be useful, I would not set my foot within his walls again.'

'But surely you would remember Marian —Mrs. Clavering's—claims on your consideration. You would remember—'

But here the inuendoes he had so unwillingly listened to in the Curzon Street drawing-room flashed across Alick's mind, and with an abruptness which bespoke his utter ignorance in the art of *mental* self-defence, he closed his judiciously-begun remarks with most suspicious suddenness.

Audaine, however, took no heed whatever of his friend's confusion, but continued, with still great vehemence, his animadversions against their host.

'He is neither more nor less than an unprincipled and dishonourable speculator, who may at any moment reduce his wife and child to beggary. I see him constantly, and have done so for long, with men of the most disreputable character, and the emotion he displayed to-night convinced me of some coming evil.'

'Then you will leave to-morrow, Ernest, and if so, so must I; but not till after breakfast, not till after we have made apologies to Mrs. Clavering.'

'So be it then,' said Ernest, not sorry, probably, of the cause which lay in Alick's urgings for the enjoyment of one more hour of Marian's society. 'So be it then, and afterwards I hope that you will be my dear old father's guest for these two days at least. I fear that you will think him aged and broken, and that—but why should I distress you with my worries? We have all our characters to play on this wide stage, and may you never, dear old friend, regret the humbler part which will soon be taken from you.'

'I shall regret it, and of that I am most certain,' responded Alick, despondingly, 'for already I look back with feverish longing to my peaceful independence, and shrink morbidly from the mortifications to which my old-fashioned ignorance will expose me.'

'You are a foolish fellow,' said Ernest, cheerfully, 'to dwell upon such trifles, and you would do well to remember the words of the poet, that—

"Honour and shame from no condition rise—
Act well your part—there all the honour lies."

And besides, there can be no earthly doubt that—unjust as it may appear—men, and indeed women likewise, are very often judged by their own evident opinion of themselves and their qualifications, for I have seen a little of this subservient, cringing world of ours, and from that little I have learnt that by a happy combination (judiciously applied) of impudence and tact, a man may always turn the tide of public opinion in his favour, and take society by storm.'

They were leaving the bright, cheerful drawing-room as Ernest closed the sentence; and as they entered the darkened inner-hall, Ernest fancied that he saw a female form flit quickly from the near neighbourhood of the door through which they had just emerged.

'How very strange,' said Alick; 'it is one o'clock; too late for women-servants to be working in the passages.'

'And too early for the housemaids to commence their broom-banging and spider-crushing,' said Ernest, cheerfully, although in a half-whisper, to his companion whose face, as he took the candle from his hand, bore even beyond its usual average of seriousness and pallor.

'How solemn the sight of that inquisitive young woman has made you, my dear Alick,' laughed Audaine; 'why, man, you have not seen a ghost, or even—God be thanked!—a lunatic,' he added, seriously. 'But now to bed, old fellow, and let us keep these various tragedies from Mrs. Clavering to-morrow, if we can.'

CHAPTER IX.

ERNEST PROVES HIMSELF A HERO.

Mrs. Clavering expressed little or no surprise at her husband's sudden disappearance; and it cannot be denied that that gentleman's absence formed an agreeable variety in her present life, and lent a greater charm to the visits she was receiving.

During Marian's wakeful hours she had meditated on her chances of persuading Ernest to reveal to her the secret which he had hitherto so carefully kept; for, as we have seen, she was piqued by his silence, and more than half-jealous of the greater amount of confidence which he had placed in Susan Brigham's discretion.

That her prudent and sensible female friend had been the one to repose an important trust in Ernest's keeping, had never once occurred to her as possible; and therefore Mrs. Clavering, being in this case ignorant of the first principles of tactics, commenced her operations under signal disadvantages.

'I must wish you Good-by immediately after breakfast, I fear,' said Ernest, looking very unsteadily away from Marian, as she poured the tea into his cup. 'I had promised my father many days ago that Harley and I would look him up, and as he has been rather ailing lately, I should not like to disappoint him.'

Marian was still quite pure of heart, and utterly incapable of building up a hope founded on her husband's absence, but still she could not bring herself to bear with perfect equanimity the loss of Ernest's greatly prized society, and on that happy day, too, when there was peace within the house, and only Alick there—good, harmless Alick—who was a friend to both, and whose useful presence prevented peril from a *tête-à-tête.*

'Must you go? I am very sorry;' and she succeeded infinitely better than he, or most men would have done, in appearing as though expressing only conventional feelings of regret. 'I am so very sorry, and I had fancied you would remain at least three days with us, Mr. Harley,' she added, turning to Alick, for tears of disappointment were beginning to glisten amongst the lashes of her dark-blue eyes. 'Mr. Harley, I hope that you will stay a little longer in this stupid house. I hope that *you* will bear me company during Mr. Clavering's absence.' And feeling that her voice began to tremble, Marian held her peace abruptly.

Breakfast was over, and Audaine, with the voice and manner of gentle authority which women often dearly love to hear and to obey, told her that as the morning was so fine, a brisk walk with him through the shrubbery would bring some roses to her cheeks, and brace her for the loneliness of the day.

She was soon ready to accompany him, and then, leaving Alick (who followed them rather sadly with his eyes), to amuse himself as best he could, he sallied forth into the wintry air.

Marian's heart beat very quickly when she found herself alone with Ernest beneath the branching sheltering evergreens, and at first she could not trust her voice to speak. But, as is almost invariably the case on such occasions, the woman took the initiative, and Marian said in a low voice—

'How cruel of you, Ernest, to desert me now—now, when thick clouds seem gathering over me! I cannot bear the storm alone, I cannot bear—'

'Hush, hush,' said Ernest in a low, hurried voice; for never before had Marian spoken to him in those imploring, tender tones, and he felt dangerously moved to pour his heart out then and there before her. 'Hush, dear,' he said, 'for you are compassed round with perils. Not only—nay do not interrupt me—

does ruin—at least I fear so—threaten to overwhelm you, but you have enemies at home, foes in your own household, spies set to watch your conduct, and put a vile construction upon all your actions.'

He spoke with haste, and even violence, for a storm of passion raged within him, and had it not found some escape in these dark warnings, he must have fallen at her feet, and sworn by all his deep devotion to be her champion in the coming battle.

Marian had been well accustomed to admiration, and gladly, and indeed eagerly, had been in the habit of encouraging the *public* attentions which men of the world are in the habit of paying to beauty and to grace; but, strange as it may appear, the situation in which she now found herself was a novel one, and past experience had not taught her how to act in an emergency like the present. There was nothing in Ernest's words to call forth any explosion either of anger or disdain. He had but spoken of her domestic troubles and of her husband's perilous speculations, which might, as she well knew—for often had Audaine warned her of the danger—bring upon herself a strange contrasting penury and discomfort.

But all the while that Marian whispered to herself that there was no hidden meaning in those eager words, an instinct known to women told her that love lurked beneath them, and that terror for her future troubles sent the wild words to Ernest's lips.

'I cannot understand you,' she replied, deceiving readily, after the manner of her sex, in moments such as these. 'Who are my foes? And who are set to spy upon me?'

'Your own maid Dawson, Marian. Aye, you may look incredulous, but why was she last night, or rather it was this morning, when your husband left the house—why was she, I say, in waiting just outside the door to listen to the words we said? She glided by me, Marian, like a spectre, but she might have spared her pains. I am not one to blurt out, even to my dearest friends, my inmost feelings—the precious secret thoughts of years, which, like a miser, I have cherished so, that I can count them with an unceasing joy, and trace a dear-loved image upon every cherished memory.'

Marian, unasked, had laid her hand on Ernest's arm, as she walked slowly and almost totteringly by his side, for a crisis in her life seemed near at hand, and now she feared her heart would prove a traitor to her head. Audaine saw at a glance how great was her emotion, and having divined its cause, hastened, by placing a check on his own passionate words, to calm the rising flood of feeling that threatened at last to break its bounds.

'I have not much time to spare, dear Marian,' he said, with a cold, evidently forced *retenue* of manner, for, like all indifferent dissemblers, his part was miserably overacted. 'I have but little time to give you, for I am due, as I before announced, this morning at my father's; but before I leave you, you must take this warning. I have for some time suspected that there is great entanglement in your husband's complicated affairs, and that at any moment he may be reduced to such uncomfortable straits that he would resort to means disastrous—or I should rather say, unpleasant—to yourself, to release him from his difficulty.'

Marian was still silent, for in truth her heart was swelling high within her under a keen sense of mortification and disappointment. She had worked herself up to the belief that a grand effort on her part, an effort which would seem the result of matronly pride and wounded dignity, was about to be required of her, and moreover she had hoped that in the hour of danger she would not be found wanting in her duty. But now, and in the place of that heroic act of self-devotion, what remained for her to do? Nothing, as it appeared to her, but to follow on as before the dull and daily routine of her tedious everyday existence, affording another example of the established truth that it is 'far more easy to act well in difficult and strongly exciting circumstances, than to fulfil correctly and patiently the wearisome duties of our daily life.' She was silent, then, under her fresh trial, for in truth she had begun to fear that the few words which, bursting from Ernest in his excitement, had thrilled so on her heart-strings, were not called forth by love for her, but for another —ah! it might be so, indeed, for Susan was Alick's near relation, and what more likely than that he might reveal to his old friend not only the secret of his love, but of that more serious confidence which he and Susan shared between them! These thoughts passed so rapidly through Marian's brain— and she had already arrived at the conclusion that in the desolation which overwhelmed her she was the most miserable of women— when Ernest, stopping suddenly in his walk, turned his eyes full upon her.

'Marian,' he said, in the low, soft whisper that ever seemed to stir the blood and life within her like 'witchcraft playing on instrumental strings.' 'Marian! listen to me, for the time has past when concealment is either profitable or possible. Listen to me, for in the midst of all your wealth and luxury you are more friendless far, and more in need of pity, than many a houseless beggar in the streets. Listen! and answer all my questions.'

'You frighten me,' murmured Marian, as, despite the chilling vapours of the now rapid thaw, he led her towards a garden seat, and placed himself beside her.

He took no notice of her half reproach, but said abruptly,—

'Do you recollect the face and figure of a man who for some years was butler in Mrs. Fletcher's house?—a tall, gray-headed man, whom she entirely trusted, but who was sent away for fraud and theft at last.'

'I do remember him quite well—his

name was Thomson; and besides, I often see him here—he comes on business, so he says, with Mr. Clavering.'

'Ha! I thought so; that will be sufficient, just at present, for my opening query. But now comes one of scarcely less importance. Was Dawson—was your maid aware that you had gone to rest last night so early? Had she any suspicion—pah! what an ugly word—that you might possibly—Marian, forgive me,' he exclaimed, for he saw an angry flush rise upwards to her forehead—'forgive me, for I would not pain you willingly—but, from many circumstances I have noticed in my visits, I fear that Dawson is your husband's spy, and that, in the belief that the low, murmured voices which she heard last night were yours and mine, she stayed to listen.'

'How miserably degrading!' exclaimed Marian. 'How cruel and undeserved! And this, then, is the recompense for well doing! Truly it is a poor reward for endeavouring to perform my irksome duties faithfully! To be watched by my own servants—to be—, oh, Ernest, do not stay a moment; who can say that even here—here, close beside us, there may not be watchful eyes and ears ready to misconstrue all we say and do.'

'Be still,' said Ernest, 'and trust all to me. During the years that I have known and loved you, Marian,'—he said the last words with a gasping sigh—'I have not been so little mindful of your interests as to fear the breath of evil tongues for you at this eleventh hour—and—'

'Why do you use such solemn words?' cried Marian, who feared she knew not what—'Why do you speak as though a doom of death, or something worse than death, were hovering over us?'

'Worse than death, indeed! For it is dishonour that I fear—dishonour for your husband, and—look the truth boldly in the face, my dearest—dishonour which must perforce react on those who bear his name.'

'Oh, Ernest!' exclaimed the unhappy woman, 'have some mercy on me—do not keep me in suspense. Give me some hint of what you mean, for I have no suspicion—believe me I have not a single clue to guide me in this matter.'

'I do, indeed, believe you—believe, and deeply feel for you. If, too, I could think it possible that my continued presence here would be a benefit, I would remain, at any risk, to—to—both of us, dear Marian—but it is not so. You scarcely yet can realize, I see, the deep-laid despicable plan which I suspect your husband has conceived; but if I should be right in my conjectures, then your house, indeed, is not a place for me, and till the horizon clears, dear love, I must see your face no more.'

'I cannot bear it,' sobbed poor Marian, who was now so utterly overcome that all plans for either words or action were forgotten, and the woman's natural feelings spoke out in uncontrollable emotion. 'I cannot bear it—I shall lose my only stay—my only comfort—' and then, seeming to recollect herself, a crimson blush covered her cheeks and brow.

Ernest rose from the bench, and taking a few turns upon the gravel walk, allowed time for both to regain some degree of composure. Marian was the first to recover herself, for, forcing back her tears, she said with tolerable calmness—

'Tell me one thing—only one—and then I will endeavour to be satisfied and patient. Has this threatened blow—this horrid bugbear, which will haunt me henceforth like an awful nightmare—has it anything to do with the murder—with the death, I mean, of Mr. Fletcher—with the secret, in short, which you and Susan Brigham share between you?'

'I fear it has,' answered Ernest, speaking in a tone so low and serious that Marian shrank instinctively from further questioning,—'I greatly fear it has; and oh, my Marian!

from this moment brace your nerves to bear the coming shocks of life with patience. I shall be near you always, although debarred the blessing of your sight. And, dearest,' he added, seeing how much she stood in need of comfort, 'is there not a true support in the reflection that we have not failed in duty or in honour, and that you can look into your little daughter's eyes and feel that you are worthy of her love?'

He rose to go, for in truth, and notwithstanding the brave words he used, there was a fierce battle going on between the flesh and spirit—between the intention to do well, and the great evil that was present with him.

She opened her lips to speak, and to catch her low, soft words, 'the very blood seemed listening in his frame.' But in vain he strained his ears for a response; no sound—at least of a syllabic meaning—came from those trembling lips, but with a smothered cry she fell upon his heart, and hiding her fair face from the pure light of heaven, wept out her sorrows there.

He smoothed the hair upon her bent-down brow, and chafed the trembling fingers in his own, and longed—oh! how he longed—to press upon her lips the first and dear-prized kiss of love and passion. But strong in his heroic and self-immolatory devotion, he strove against the fierce temptation, and—all praise to his brave heart—he came forth a conqueror.

An hour after this trying scene—a scene which sent Marian, with a heart anxious, yet half-guiltily consoled, to bear her solitude as best she might—the friends were journeying onward through the bleak New-year's air towards a pretty neighbouring villa, where for many years Admiral Audaine, now almost an octogenarian, but still both hale and fresh of heart, received the visits of his many friends, and (greatly prized above them all) that of his only son. They touched on many topics as they rode along, but not on one connected with the thoughts that filled their minds.

And so they reached the cottage (for it *was* one to all intents and purposes), and there beneath the pretty porch, they saw the kind old man, who, with his white hairs glistening in the sun like threads of silver, came forth to bid them welcome with a glow of pleasure on his withered cheeks.

CHAPTER X.

ERNEST AUDAINE IN DIFFICULTIES.

It has now become necessary (although I must throw myself upon the merciful consideration of my Court of Readers to pardon what may appear in the light of another digression)—it has now become—in my own opinion—necessary to touch lightly upon some of Ernest Audaine's peculiar characteristics, as well as to allude *en passant* to the rather singular worldly position in which he stood. It has been said, or at least implied, that he was not addicted to low vices. From these his inborn refinement, which caused him to shrink from contact with the coarse and sensual, had happily preserved him; but though saved by his own more delicate tastes and habits from the contamination of vicious society, there existed for him other, and no less dangerous temptations—temptations to which he had, in his earlier days, yielded with scarcely an effort at resistance.

Endowed with a keen appreciation for—nay, I may almost call it an idolatry—of the beautiful, it had been his misfortune, and that not seldom, to worship at those shrines where costly offerings must be laid before the altars of their idols. We may blame him if we will, and if our conscience tells us we may throw a stone at this weak son of Adam, why let us begin, in Heaven's name, the pleasant work of lapidation. But should a whispering voice remind us that we too are human, then let us cast around for those who shared his sin, but not its punishment—for those whose eager craving after pleasure and whose all-insatiate vanity had power to lead a very boy in years—a child indeed to *them* in worldly knowledge—into those dangerous excesses which brought upon him, in his middle age, a heavy punishment.

Ernest was very young when he (as it is called) 'got into his first scrape.' He was by nature chivalrous, and, to a certain extent, self-sacrificing. What wonder, then, that on him alone fell the reprobation that followed, or the scandal which ensued?

His father, kind, and to a certain extent, unprincipled—for he acknowledged *no* law but that of honour—was not startled into severity by his son's imprudence. He did not foresee that having once tasted of the poisoned cup of excitement, Ernest *could* not abstain from the dangerous draught; nor did he calculate on the many and terrible evils that would ensue when the moral drunkenness should become a chronic and an habitual malady. And so the years rolled on—years during which the unthinking boy lavished the best gifts of his young affections on the vain, the interested, and the unworthy!

Plunged in those inextricable errors, during their continuance in which, since the world began, men have never seen the 'serpent locks' that rise above a lovely woman's face, he was ever, 'with a mad surprise,' hastening like the moth that hies after a taper, and burning his bright wings in the treacherous flame.

But there were other evils attendant on this course of life (for the pursuit of dangerous pleasure had alarmingly soon become a *habit* with Ernest), besides the almost certain deterioration of his principles, and even of his very nature.

'Il y a des heures où une femme est assez heureuse lorsqu'elle se sent enviée par toutes ses rivales,' and the world has not now to learn how insatiable is the passion of which the Frenchman writes, or how perilous to the feeder of it, is often that desperate and eager craving.

Many, it is to be feared, were the ruinous victories thus obtained by Ernest Audaine; and it was in the doubtful enjoyment of them that much of the time that should have been devoted to study and mental improvement passed away. The dangerous consequences of his early follies were long undreamt of by their perpetrator; but there comes a time in the life of even the most light-hearted and unthinking when conscience, roused to wakefulness by a dread of personal annoyances, speaks at last, and will perforce be heard. This time had come at last for Ernest, and many were the anxious hours he spent in vain regrets for the past, and in equally useless calculations on the ways and means for the retrieving of his shattered fortunes. Both the Admiral and Alick took note of the change which had of late come over his spirits, and commented on it sadly in their hearts, when missing the pleasant accents of his cheerful voice, and the joyous ring of his once happy laugh.

They formed no surmises as to the cause of what they saw, for both shrunk from prying even in spirit into his secrets; but still they longed for the moment when the overburdened spirit would spontaneously pour forth its confession and claim the sympathy they were yearning to bestow.

For several years—years during which the anxieties and inconveniences entailed on Ernest by his early imprudences had certainly not decreased in number and oppressiveness—for several years, then, Ernest had been in the habit of indulging his own filial feelings, and of benefiting his friend, by encouraging the latter to accept with him of the Admiral's cordially-offered hospitalities. It was a very charming country home that in which Ernest visited his aged father, and where Alick—whose previous life had not been marked with many blessings—learnt to believe that there is a blessing in the mere boon of life which God has given to all. It was the day after their hurried departure from Craven Bank, and Ernest had gone out walking, for a spring-like morning had followed on the thaw, and the smooth-shaved lawn that sloped down to the river was all bathed in sunshine. The shadows were growing long, however, now—and the Admiral was standing before the large French window and watching for his son's return. The letters that, since he left them three hours before, had arrived by the Post for Ernest, were lying in a heap upon the table; but no one had examined them. There had been no glance to see the nature of the handwriting, nor the impression of the Post-stamp—for the loyal old man trusted his son entirely, and, except for his own happiness, entertained not the shadow of a misgiving.

At last a step was heard upon the gravel, and Ernest, with a wearied look, approached the window.

'Not late, is it, my dear father?' he asked, adding, with all his wonted courtesy, 'Alick, I beg your pardon; I went further than I thought, before I turned to come home. Letters! Oh, how I hate the sight of them!' and glancing at most of those he had received without even opening them, he thrust them into his pocket.

Of one, however, he did break the seal, and after hastily running his eye over its contents, an exclamation of surprise, and something very like an oath, escaped his lips.

'What is the matter? No bad news, I trust,' asked his father, anxiously.

'Good enough for the old lunatic himself, perhaps,' muttered Ernest, 'but bad rather for us. Had you any idea, sir,' he added, more directly addressing the Admiral, 'that Lord Clanboyne was going to be married?'

'Married—impossible!'

'I wish with all my heart that I could take your view of the case; but, on the contrary, I believe that every man, at some period or other of his life, is absurd enough to perpetrate matrimony. My good uncle (oh, my prophetic soul!) has done so at last. I always thought he would, so my chances in life are over;' and he sighed gloomily.

Alick looked up in surprise. 'Surely,' he said to himself, 'it cannot be the loss of a coronet' (for hitherto, in right of his mother,

Ernest had been heir presumptive to a barony) 'that calls forth such evidence of regret;' and fearing that there must exist some deeper cause for Audaine's depression, he half resolved to question him on the subject when they should be alone.

'But, my dear Ernest,' began the old man, who as yet could not bring himself to believe in the reality of the blow (and it *was* a severe one) that had fallen upon them, 'do tell me from whom you have heard this news—I can hardly believe it—surely we must have heard of—'

'If my uncle had married what is called a "proper person," it is just possible that he might have condescended to prepare us for the calamity; but as the blushing bride he has led to the hymenial altar is—but never mind —there'll be a son as sure as—I shall have to blow my brains out'—muttered he to himself. 'But here's the paper, sir, with the announcement. It came enclosed to me. And now hadn't we better be thinking of dinner—I believe it is seven o'clock. Heigh-ho!' and with another wearied sigh he left the room.

It was the Admiral's habit to retire early to rest, and his departure was usually the signal for a more unreserved communion of thoughts between Ernest and his friend, but on this occasion, to the latter's surprise and regret, there was constraint between them, the while they sat musingly in their lounging chairs before the fire, gazing into its hot depths, and carefully avoiding the meeting of each other's eyes.

Harley was the first to break the silence, saying in a low voice, 'Your father seemed very uneasy this evening at your late return.'

'Did he? dear old man! Alick, I greatly fear that his uneasiness about me is but just beginning. The truth is, that I'm in such confounded difficulties!'

'Difficulties!' repeated Alick, in alarm, 'what difficulties?'

'Why, what could they be, except as regards money, you foolish fellow! And mine have been grinding on so long now! renewing bills, and all that kind of business. Things you know about as much of as the man in the moon, and you may thank your stars, or rather your excellent self, that so it is. You can't guess what I've gone through—I couldn't tell you—I never did'—and this was true enough, for Ernest, with all his reckless disregard of public opinion, had kept the friend, whose ignorance of the world he respected while he pitied it, utterly in the dark on the subject of his least excusable errors. Alick had, perhaps, a right to feel gratified by that reticence, viewing it as a just, though tacit tribute to the religious principles of which he did not *dare* to seem ashamed.

For a few minutes he pondered sadly over his friend's words, and then said—

'Your father cannot dream of this, I'm sure, dear Ernest, and it does not seem as though you should with him have any concealments.'

'No concealments! And what do you

think would be the consequence of my confiding in him? Why he'd starve himself to pay my debts: and that he sha'n't do—by ——.'

'Still he ought to know,' persisted Alick; but Ernest interrupted him vehemently.

'I have had these cursed Jews,' he said, '(Barabbasses every one of them) at me for a year past. They were only kept quiet by the belief that I should succeed to my uncle; and now the old fool's married, of course they're rampant. There should be a law against old men making asses of themselves. It's immoral—it's ob—'

'Hush,' said Alick, quietly, 'there's no use in raging now it's over, and besides, I think I've an idea—you don't know it,' he added (and he could not help growing hot and red), 'but I have plenty of money.

'You? Come now, Alick, look me in the face and repeat that same.'

'Yes, I can—for I have more money now than I can find uses for—money that Lord

Ashington has given me for my wedding outfit. I can find no way of spending this five hundred pounds, and if you will only take it—you, to whom I owe so much—you, who—'

'Take it, my dear fellow! Rob you of your little all! Why what a cur you must consider me!'

'But it is not little—and if you won't have all, at least take some—enough to pay the largest and most pressing creditors. Surely you will not refuse me.'

The reader can well understand how that Ernest, comparing the thousands that he owed, with the paltry hundreds that seemed to his inexperienced friend so all-sufficient to meet the exigencies of the case, would have smiled had that friend been less ignorant and simple-minded than the slow-witted Alick; but being what he was, tears instead of merriment glistened in the spendthrift's eyes.

'My dear good fellow,' he said, as he pressed his hand affectionately, 'how little you know of how much a man may, without great difficulty, contrive to owe! Why, five times five hundred would not set me clear.'

Alick looked aghast, but Ernest would not give him time to express his surprise.

'I hardly know how it all began,' he said, musingly. 'I think it was partly Harry Denhurst's fault, for he couldn't stand, no more could I, seeing that horrid fellow, Topham, hoarding up his money, and it was so jolly to make him fork out! I almost wish, though, that I had never had anything to do with that set. No, I don't—it was such fun.'

'The fun is over now,' suggested Alick, gravely.

'Yes, and exactly contrary to the "baseless fabric" of a vision, *has* left a *wreck* behind.'

'But wouldn't Clavering lend the money?' said Harley, brightening up at the idea.

'Clavering lend! In the first place, if I were starving I would not ask him; and in the next—but this is said in confidence—I believe the Jew to be on the brink of worse than ruin; and, if I mistake not, he will wake some morning and find himself infamous! Alick, that man's entire soul is in a balance at his bankers! His very finger-ends itch for gold. The sound of its clink is his best-beloved music, and the scent of a dirty five-pound note is more savoury in his nostrils than the choicest perfumes of Araby the Blest. And now,' he added with a laugh, 'have I not proved most satisfactorily that the senses which lead other men astray, are not even as *his* senses are?'

Alick was amused for a moment by his pleasantries, but they failed to turn him from his purpose—a purpose in which he was at last successful—namely, that of convincing Ernest that there was no kindness in concealment, and that the *certainty* of the worst was better for his indulgent and anxious parent than the suspense he had lately been enduring.

CHAPTER XI.

HOW JEMMY GRAYTON SLEPT WITH BOTH EYES SHUT.

THE progress of our story taking us at this point once more amongst the humbler ranks of society, I must request my readers to follow me again to Jemmy Grayton's suburban cottage, in which unobtrusive dwelling he will find our old and diminutive reprobate acquaintance, Amelius Driver. It would appear from various changes noticeable in the conduct and habits of that young gentleman, that he had latterly become profitably impressed with the necessity for some improvement both in his outer and his inner man. As regarded the first, his early efforts at personal adornment had been crowned with a very partial success; for the cheap article in the shape of a very bright blue silk cravat which encircled his thin throat, and the mock carbuncle that fastened the same, were far from adding to the already not over-distinguished appearance of Carry Driver's son. That feeble-minded, but deeply-repentant woman had seen with regret her own taste for meretricious finery inherited by her offspring, and had endeavoured, but in vain, to turn the lad's attention to other and more prudent modes for the investment of his limited capital. But Yussy, as is the case with many shabby-looking little fellows in this ambitious world of ours, thought to make amends for personal deficiencies by smart clothes and shining jewels—a weakness which increased upon him rapidly, as the means of gratifying it came within his reach.

But, as I have said, it was not on his outward improvement alone that Mr. Amelius Driver had begun to lavish unwonted care and attention. He had become disagreeably aware of his many mental and educational shortcomings; and when he contrasted them with the brilliant prospects held out to him by Thomson—(prospects which, though evidently far away in the dim vista of futurity, were for ever glimmering, brightly as a glow-worm in a dusky night, before his eyes)—he resolved to devote all his leisure hours, of which the young gentleman had many, to rendering himself more suited to the exalted station which he expected at some future day to fill.

Education is a boon which is not always to be had for nothing; but the persevering searcher for it under difficulties will sometimes find his efforts crowned with some success. There are a few good people in the world who take delight in teaching the young idea how to shoot, and not a few whose vanity is gratified by showing tyros their own superior erudition. Of these two classes of individuals, the one that Amelius fortunately lighted on, belonged without a question to the first; for Mr. Grayton, out of pure friendship as it seemed to the boy's weak mother, had volunteered to become his 'guide, philosopher, and friend.'

The distance from London—a good half-hour by rail—might have appeared to Yussy an almost insurmountable objection to the plan proposed by Grayton (namely, that the lad should come to him three times a week for lessons), had not the excellent and liberal rate-collector offered, from his own pocket, to defray the third-class fare expense attendant on the journeys to and fro.

'I don't think anything of the money, my dear,' said Grayton to his wife, who, kind-hearted as she was, had ventured on a mild remonstrance. 'He that giveth to the poor, you know, lendeth to the Lord.'

'Yes; that is very true; but still there is the child, to think of—and your long illness, James. Why, only for the doctor's kindness we should be in dreadful trouble now. That bill for twenty pounds that we still owe to

Dr. Collins is often a sore drag upon me. And, though I'm very sorry for Mrs. Driver and her sister, we should be just before we're generous.'

'All right, my little woman,' broke in Grayton, cheerfully. 'You needn't be afraid of my extravagance; and I am not the man that would forget the child, or you, my dear, or even the bills we've got to pay, although they're not a pleasant subject to remember.'

She was a very unsuspecting little woman, or long ere this she would have guessed that there existed some other cause (besides his pity for the unhappy and disappointed mother) which worked such charity in Grayton's breast towards the graceless son. She knew her husband to be warm of heart, and had never since her marriage found him deficient in the wish to give, according to his means, to those who were in want. He was a man, too (and of that she never doubted), whose rectitude of conduct, and whose unswerving honesty were above all praise; and so she trusted him, and bore, as best she might, the constant presence of that, to her, unpleasant-looking object in the trim, cheerful kitchen of her humble dwelling. The boy is seated at the small deal table now, with a much-thumbed, dirty copy-book spread out before him, on which Yussy, with his shaggy head bent low upon the page, is tracing slowly, and with labouring fingers, some great round O's, the joinings of whose rebellious circles appears a task impossible to accomplish.

Grayton, whose health is scarcely yet restored, for he has been a terrible sufferer from that fell disease lumbago, is stretched out, newspaper in hand, on the old-fashioned, high-backed chair to which, as master of the house, he is indubitably entitled. His attention every now and then being turned towards the youthful scribe, whose long, unhealthy-looking fingers, on which a plenteous crop of warts is flourishing, are struggling manfully with the intricacies of caligraphy.

'Hold your pen straight, there's a good

lad,' said Mr. Grayton, for at least the thousandth time since those inauspicious lessons had begun. 'Hold your pen straight, and lean on the down strokes. Why, man, you'll never make a writer if you go on in this way;' and snatching, with some natural impatience, the pen from his pupil's hand, the Rate Collector set himself to the far more easy task of demonstrating by example, that the letter O should be turned up at the bottom in a graceful curve, and end in a neat flourish at the top.

'Oh my! how tiresome it is,' said Yussy, with a sonorous sigh, as his instructor, pushing back the copy-book before him, showed him what the letter *ought* to look like. 'It's precious tiresome, this is. I say—couldn't one learn of fellows that put advertisements in the papers, and say they'll make you write in half-a-dozen lessons?'

'Well, you could, but then I can't help thinking they don't learn you thoroughly; and besides—'

'Law, Yussy!' put in Ellen, jealous for her husband, 'law, Yussy! you are not a-going to say you think that anyone could learn you better than my James? It's only just to try a little. Why, you are getting on. A week ago you couldn't write your name; and now here it is—Amelius Driver—just as pat as anythink.'

The lad looked up, encouraged, in the woman's kindly face. He was not used to praise; for at his home in that dull alley where he lived, his mother, with her face of constant gloom, seemed ever standing between him and hopeful thoughts. She was an unwitting kill-joy, nor did she guess how much her pensive face, added to her boy's dislike to home, had fostered and confirmed his evil habits; but Ellen guessed the truth, and knowing from experience what a light a woman's pleasant smile sends gleaming o'er a darkening hearth, she tried her favourite remedy's effect upon the widow's son, and found it answer.

'I want to write,' said Yussy, 'but I hate these pens. I like a quill; this makes my fingers ache.'

'Ellen, my dear,' said Grayton, looking up from the Penny Paper thoughtfully, 'you're going out, you said. Suppose you buy some pens, they're always useful. Here's a shilling, and the rest in lollipops for Nelly.'

'My gracious, James! Sure what a man you are! Why it was only yesterday that you spent a shilling on the little poppet, and now it's to be done again. Well, well! it isn't my fault if you spoil her;' and Mrs. Grayton, with a look of intense maternal satisfaction in her comely face, betook herself upstairs to make her darling ready for the walk.

No sooner did Amelius find himself alone with his instructor, than he began again to fidget on his chair, and look as though he were dissatisfied with the materials on which he had to work.

'Well, what's the matter now, boy?' demanded Grayton, rather peevishly, for he was growing sleepy by the warm, bright fire-light, and Yussy's *wrigglings* disturbed him not a little.

'I want some other paper now,' replied the boy. 'I promised a friend of mine to send him my direction, and if you'd write it for me I could take it with me when I go.'

Grayton, who was really good-natured, and was, moreover, easily aroused when business, however trifling, was in question, set himself to work at once to find the articles demanded by his pupil.

'We don't do much of letter-writing here,' he said, 'and all the stationery's locked up inside the desk. But here's the key among my watch-keys, and you can look yourself. The writing paper's in the upper part. That's it, and now lock up again, my boy. That's right; and put the watch down on the table. Lord, Lord, how sleepy this hot fire makes me.'

And having so said, the worthy rate-collector laid himself back in his chair, and before a minute had elapsed, was snoring loudly.

Meanwhile, the ponderous silver watch, with its huge seal and brazen key were lying near the desk, in which receptacle, as Yussy knew full well, his teacher kept his secret and most valued papers. The dwarf's keen and cunning eyes were fixed upon it wistfully, and anon they turned with eagerness to watch the breathing of the slumbering man, who might at any instant rouse himself, and guess why *he* stood there in trembling silence; for it was true that every limb and fibre of the agitated lad had, since those last few minutes, vibrated like an aspen leaf; and had the mistress of the house chanced to return at that strange juncture, the chances would have been greatly in favour of her running at once to Dr. Collins, and asking his advice concerning the sudden malady with which her guest had been assailed. It was not the first time by many an one that the chance of being alone (so to speak) with that old, dark, mahogany writing-desk had seemed, indeed, a 'golden opportunity' to the deeply-scheming dwarf; and now—and after many a day of waiting and disappointment—his most sanguine expectations were almost fulfilled! True, he was not alone, for close beside the object of his en-wrapt attention slept its unsuspecting owner, whilst, ere he could have time to execute the project he had formed, the mistress of the house might make her re-appearance, and frustrate by her unwelcome presence the long-cherished object of his life. Still, and notwithstanding these alarming hindrances to success, Amelius did not hesitate as to his plan of operations.

'Nothing venture, nothing have,' he murmured to himself, and then, with a rapid recollection of how few had hitherto been his opportunities, and how little probable it was that any future occasion more propitious than the present would be accorded to him by his unbounteous stars, he prepared to tempt his fate at once.

Happily for his chances of success, the high-backed chair on which Mr. Grayton was soundly sleeping was so placed that the shoulders of its occupant, and not his face, were turned towards the scene of operation. That his slumbers, too, were little likely to be disturbed by any trifling noise was evident from the loud and regular respirations which came at intervals from that place of calm repose. Very re-assuring were those nasal tokens of unconsciousness to the unscrupulous Yussy, as he laid his fingers stealthily on the chain and seals, which, thanks to the exceeding tenderness with which he handled them, gave forth no betraying sound. His next task—and it was one of considerable difficulty—was to insert the key into its place and turn it noiselessly. He was not new to tricks of this description, for, in anticipation of the present crisis, he had practised (and that under an able master) the useful art of 'fingering' dexterously, and his sleight-of-hand did him good service now.

In seeking out the especial paper for which he ran this terrible risk, Amelius neither anticipated nor did he meet with difficulty. He had often been a witness to the spreading out upon the table of the contents of Jemmy Grayton's desk, for the latter, in his capacity of rate-collector had, of course, like other official characters, his accounts to keep in order. And thus it happened that the outward aspect of one carefully sealed-up document was perfectly familiar to that skilful depredator.

A minute only had elapsed since the bad boy commenced his treacherous work, and already his thin fingers were diving among the littering papers, the time-worn letters, packets of tied-up receipts, and other 'rubbish,' as the searcher deemed them, but which were doubtless by the worthy parish-officer deemed of the most vital public interest. With a muttered curse (that natural but terrible expansion of the feelings even of those who are still young in crime), Amelius thrust aside the impediments in his way, and at last, and to his unbounded joy, the sight of three large black seals was the reward of his exertions. He took the packet on which these seals were impressed hastily from its hiding-place, and thrust it beneath his shirt-front with a hand that slightly shook, so great was his excitement. The crowning deed was scarcely quite achieved, however, when a shadow fell across the floor, and Yussy, guessing rightly that it heralded the return of Mrs. Grayton, pushed the scattered papers hurriedly (and without the least regard to their previously neat arrangement) into the desk, and locking it with a celerity which was a marvel in itself, he flung himself upon his seat, one second only before the opening door gave entrance to the mother and her child.

'What, sleeping, James!' exclaimed the cheerful woman, whose bright red cheeks were shining with good humour and the effects of the brisk, frosty air without. 'Here, Nelly, wake your father up, my child; and Master Yussy, help to clear the table, for we must get our dinners, and maybe you will take your own along with us to-day.'

But Amelius was in far too great a hurry to escape from the scene of his delinquency to accept this hospitable offer. He knew, as well as if a glass reflected them, that his cheeks were deadly pale, and that the hands he hid beneath the table were still trembling violently; so, making, with the best face he could a plausible excuse, the wretched tool of others and his own selfish passions crept from his benefactor's house with shaking limbs, but a triumphant heart.

For on his breast, he nothing doubted, lay the talisman of his fortunes, and what was, perhaps, well nigh as precious to the heart, the instrument of vengeance on the pair who, since his earliest infancy, had thwarted and oppressed him.

CHAPTER XII.

MR. GRAYTON RECEIVES A BLOW.

ALTHOUGH Jemmy Grayton had often been an ailing man—and, indeed, perhaps because he had, in gossip's parlance, 'enjoyed' so long a feeble state of health—the quondam lawyer's-clerk felt no misgiving concerning his own probably very limited length of days; nor did his habitual maladies cause any great amount of anxiety in the breast of his busy wife. She had long acted the part of nurse towards one who, from the mere fact of his being so much her senior, she had made up her mind from the first, was to be by her, tended, comforted, and almost protected. Ellen had never felt for a moment wearied by the sleepless, watchful nights which, when Mr. Grayton was laid up with 'rheumatiz,' she was obliged to pass by his bedside; but then, as she was wont to say, 'James was one of a thousand, and never from year's end to year's end did he say one word to her that was louder than another.'

On the morning after the depredation—so long and so cunningly planned—had been perpetrated by Amelius Driver, the self-elected tutor of that unpromising young gentleman awoke from a refreshing sleep, and told his wife he had not felt so well for years.

'I feel as lissom,' he remarked, 'as lissom as I did at twenty. I could collect the rates to-day myself, my dear, and no occasion to give money to a deputy. What's the weather like to-day, Ellen? The east wind's gone, I'm sure; I feel that in my bones.'

'Gone, aye, that it is, father,' answered Ellen; 'a morning like the spring; and there's a robin singing on the upper gooseberry bush, and Nelly holding out the crumbs to him—the darling!'

They were a very happy little party at that simple breakfast-table! To be sure, there was no bright array of plate and china, but a good metal tea-pot—Ellen never allowed that tea would draw in *chayney*—and everything as clean as human hands could make it.

How Grayton did enjoy his breakfast on that spring-like morning, with the robin peering in upon them from the window-sill, and little Nelly's rosy mouth making sweet chirrups to the saucy bird, who nodded his bright head, and seemed to do his best to answer her.

'I should think a walk would do you good to-day, father,' suggested Ellen, 'and you can take Nelly out into the sun, and let her toddle just a little bit—the precious!'

'All right,' said Grayton, cheerfully; 'and afterwards I'll go about that long arrears of Mrs. Mason's. I mightn't feel so well another time to do it.'

'No; nor the day to suit so well,' added

his wife. 'So now, my pet, let's go and put its bonnet on, and it shall walk with father round the garden, and see the pretty dicky-birds, and neighbour Coley's itty-itty bow-wow.'

And so the mother went out with her child, talking to it in foolish infant language suited to its tender years. She watched the father and his child along the garden-walk with something of a woman's pride in both, for Grayton, although turned of fifty, was still, when not distressed by illness, what Ellen called 'quite a fine figure of a man;' and then his dress was always neat and clean, so that some people—not good judges doubtless—had been known to fall into mistakes, and take the rate-collector for a gentleman. She watched them from the parlour-window as little Nelly's tiny steps went pattering on the narrow gravel walk, the while her hand was held so tightly in that broad, strong palm, that the child almost felt inclined to say it gave her pain.

He was so careful of his little daughter—that man whose early life had been fraught with great temptation to small sins—that her every step was guarded by him for fear the pebble in her path should prove a stumbling-block, and any evil, chance to Ellen's child. And still the mother watched them from the window in her pride, and still, upon the sunny path the infant and the man of middle age came slowly on.

It was strange—but in after-days, and when quickly-succeeding circumstances tended to impress that winter's walk upon her memory—it was strange how every small detail connected with that morning's exercise returned on Ellen Grayton's mind. They had been half-an-hour in that humble garden, walking betwixt the leafless gooseberry-bushes, and viewing with interest, doubtless, the drooping, frost-bitten cabbage-plants that were the only edible vegetables visible at that inclement season, when Ellen, seeing a tired look upon her little darling's face, and noticing that she dragged against the hand that held her own, beckoned to Grayton to bring the child in doors.

'Why, sure,' said Jemmy, as he handed Nelly to her mother, 'sure you can't be thinking that the little lassie's tired. But it's such a fine warm day, that I must take advantage of it to go about my business. Fetch me the keys, my dear, for I must look up all the papers, and have it all ship-shape before Inspection-day.'

He was so hearty in his speech, and looked so fresh and vigorous, that Ellen almost fancied he had grown young again; and with that thought her spirits rose, and as she went to do his bidding, she sung upon the narrow stairs a snatch of song that came from her heart's gladness.

He took the keys, and thanked her, for there was a kind of in-born courtesy in that low-born man that, more than all the rest, perhaps, kept love alive for him in Ellen's breast. He took the keys, and sitting down before the desk prepared to make up his accounts. Ellen was busied in her household matters; she always was when little Nelly slept, for that young tyrant threw her parent's work sometimes into arrears. Well, she was busied with her household duties, and took no heed of the good man, whose head—now thickly sprinkled with the gray hairs which, as the proverb says, are Death's first warning—was bent over his scattered papers. She went to and fro with a light spirit on which no shadow of a coming event had power to throw its gloom, whilst ever and anon she stole upstairs to look at Nelly sleeping, and draw the curtain with a careful hand to shield her darling from the cold.

It was on returning from one of these maternal expeditions that she heard her name called out (in a sharp, high tone, very different from his usual mild accosting) by her husband.

'Coming, dear; coming in one moment!' called out Ellen. And then it was—'Oh, dear, we shall awake the child;' but still she hurried down, and in a moment more she stood by Grayton's side.

She looked with wonder at his altered face, at the wild look that glared from his wide-open eyes, and at the leaden hue that had usurped the place of his fresh morning colour.

'Why, Grayton, dear,' she said, 'why, father! What on earth's the matter?'

'Matter!' he cried, 'matter enough to drive me mad: matter enough to hang—no, no, not that, but still a frightful loss, my dear—a frightful loss indeed!' The latter words were said something more gently, for he had looked up in Ellen's frightened eyes, and feared just then to try her further.

She drew a lengthened breath—it might be of relief—for his last words, in contrast with the first, were almost re-assuring. And then, taking a wooden chair that stood against the wall, she placed it close beside him, and sitting down, began her questioning.

'What's lost, my dear?' she asked; 'sure not the paper that you was speaking of this morning? not what was wanted about Mrs. Mason, surely?'

'Mrs. Mason! Pshaw! What's Mrs. Mason, I should like to know, when—oh, my dear!' he added, feelingly, for his momentary irritation gave way at once at sight of her grieved face, 'oh, my dear, this is a dreadful business, for I have lost that which—ah, me! I cannot say to you what shame and misery this may bring upon us; shame—black and lasting upon me—and misery—aye, and utter poverty upon you and Nelly!'

Ellen was not a woman of many words; it may be said, too, that her ideas were scant in quantity, and not remarkable for their originality. Hers also was not a cultivated mind; and her education, beyond the humblest learning taught in a village school, was nothing. But Mrs. Grayton, to counterbalance these striking disadvantages, was endowed in no inconsiderable degree with the rare gift of common-sense, a quality which, as we must all agree, is frequently so much more useful in the emergencies of life than what are called the 'higher gifts of genius and of talent.' She was mentally brave, too, far braver than her husband; for where *he* would wait and temporize, letting 'I dare not wait upon I would,' till the time for profitable action passed away, *she* would, on the contrary, go stoutly forth to meet the danger, and would often, by opposing, end it.

She followed on this occasion the dictates of her own calm, quiet sense, by deciding that Grayton must be at once induced to confide the secret, whatever it might be, to one who was at once his guide, his consoler, and the chief prop of his declining years.

She did not startle him by her first leading question, but said with simple earnestness—

'What was the paper like, my dear? You may have overlooked it, as I have done a score o' times with things I couldn't lay my hands on. What was it like? Let's have another look; James, dear:' and as she spoke she laid her hand upon the scattered papers near her.

He pushed it softly back from off the table, and leaning back despondingly, said in a low husky voice—

'There isn't any use in looking, Ellen. The packet that I have kept for years within that desk is gone to-day, and I'm a ruined man—God help me!'

'What was it like to look at?' Ellen asked.

'Like? Why that can matter very little now; however, it has ceased to be a secret. It was a small thin packet, sealed with black.'

'Had it three seals upon it?'

'It had—what then?' he eagerly inquired, while looking up for some good token in her placid eyes.

'Only that scarce a week ago I saw it in the desk there; and, James, who *could* have touched it since? We've never been away, you know, we two at once. And then, the keys; why don't they always hang up with the watch, at night upon the tester? No, Grayton, take my word it's there. Law, dear, who would think to find a thing at once in all that clutter? It's foolishness to think it wouldn't get mislaid.'

Grayton still leant back upon his high-backed chair, and the fixed gloom upon his countenance deepened beneath her hopeful words.

'You may look, of course, my dear,' he said, 'but it is only waste of time; yes, it is only waste of time.'

Glad of the permission, Ellen commenced a rigorous search amongst the various documents that lay strewed, not only on the table, but on the sanded floor, where they had fallen during Grayton's hurried, nervous investigation. Jemmy looked on in silence. He was supported by none of that sanguine hope which encouraged his cheerful-tempered wife, to turn over every scrap of scattered paper, with the vain expectation that in the end some good might follow on her labour; for he had been at least as careful as poor Ellen in his investigations, and knew full well how useless was the task she had imposed upon herself.

It was over at last, that vain and profitless research; and Mrs. Grayton, with a hot, flushed face and trembling hands—for she had been eager in her work—rested from her labour, and took to serious conjecturing.

'Well, my dear?' said Jemmy meaningly, after a lengthened pause, which rather tried his patience.

'Well, James,' responded Ellen thoughtfully. 'You'll think it odd, I know, and maybe call me foolish; but I've got a thought—a thought that's come into my head within these ten minutes, and that is—now, don't you go and cry it down without considering—'

'I won't, my dear; I won't. Two heads are better often than a man's alone, so, now for your idea—not that I hope much from it —not I; for I'm a ruined man, my dear—a wretched, ruined man.'

Ellen took no notice of these reiterated exclamations, so engrossed was she by the new surmises with which her brain was labouring. At last, however, and precisely at the moment when her husband was opening his mouth again to sue for an explanation, the result of the wife's cogitations became apparent.

'James,' she began—and there was something almost deprecating in her tone—'James, you have sometimes blamed me, dear, because I couldn't cotton to that boy you have encouraged here. To Carry Driver's son, I mean. Well! I was wrong, perhaps, but still, I couldn't help it; for, to my mind, there's something impish in the lad. I wouldn't trust him, James. I wouldn't let him be alone with anything I valued. I wouldn't—no, I wouldn't let him kiss our Nelly for a thousand pounds!'

She had arrived at the climax now, for the expression of her antipathy could no further go, and the while that Grayton looked upon her wonderingly, she paused to recover her breath and her composure.

'It is my belief, Grayton,' she said, when this result had in some sort been arrived at, 'it is my belief—may God forgive me if I wrong him; but it's my belief that 'Melius Driver had a hand in taking off that paper.'

Mr. Grayton, whose attention had gradually been diverted from Ellen's suggestions by the quickly-rising memories which whispered awful warnings to his frightened conscience, turned round quite sharply in his chair as Ellen spoke.

'Why, wife,' he said; 'what put that fancy in your head? Amelius Driver take it! Gracious me! What should the boy want with it? What should he know of—of—of its worth to him? What should—Ellen, my dear, my heart is painful—very painful—the old, old pain that I remember.'

And as the trembling words came slowly from his lips, his wife could see a faintly livid hue spread over all his features.

She helped him up the stairs, and to the bed, on which he lay outside the patchwork coverlid. 'He would not see the doctor,' so he said, 'but Ellen would keep watch beside him,'—which she did for many a weary hour, whilst all the time the feeble moans broke forth; and Jemmy Grayton muttered often—'he took his own—yes—he but took his own. May God forgive me for my sin!'

CHAPTER XIII.

ELLEN SHARES THE BURDEN.

JEMMY GRAYTON never closed his eyes throughout the weary night that followed on his dread discovery, and when the morning came, Ellen was frightened at the change which those few hours of suffering had wrought upon his frame.

She had not left him for a moment till the morning dawned, and then she hastened down to make the cup of tea—poor Grayton's favourite restorative—the which she fondly hoped would work its usual wonders now.

The pure, fresh morning air blew upon Ellen's face as she stood out for one brief instant on the door-step. The sun had scarcely fully risen, although from out his brilliant bed, where—

> 'Brought forth in purple, cradled in vermillion,
> Baptized in moulten gold, and swathed in dun,'

he seemed to linger still;—the god of day was mounting slowly upwards to his duty in the sky.

The sight, beautiful although it was, failed for the first time within her memory to awaken feelings of gratitude and admiration in the breast of her who gazed upon it. But the truth was that Ellen's heart was very heavy. Not that illness in the case of Mr. Grayton was (as I have said) a new event to her, but that a grievous weight—the sure presentiment of coming evil—crushed down her accustomed buoyant spirits and warned her that she had fallen upon evil days.

'How happy we were yesterday,' murmured the troubled woman, with that strange pertinacity which prompts us ever to contrast the brighter past with the dull, lowering present. 'How happy we were yesterday;' and then her thoughts flew back to Nelly in the sun-lit garden, with her father holding the tiny hand in his, and guiding the child's tottering footsteps tenderly.

The tears rose up in Mrs. Grayton's eyes as the pleasant vision rose before her, and then reproaching herself for that sad waste of time, she turned away to find in active work a remedy for all her sorrows.

'Do take a sup, James, dear,' she said, a short while after, as she presented herself cup in hand by the sick man's bedside. 'I made it strong a'purpose. Just a little sup, to do you good.'

He raised himself, and tried to do her bidding, but the warm liquid seemed to choke him, and setting down poor Ellen's well-meant offering, he fell back on his pillow with a stifling sigh. It was a desperate case, so the poor woman thought, and therefore desperate remedies were lawful. Desperate, indeed, for Ellen's fixed-on recipe was nothing less severe than to speak strongly to her husband at this crisis, urging him by all his love for her and for his child, and (what appeared of more important moment) by his sworn duty to his Maker and his neighbour, to reveal the whole amount of what he feared might chance to him.

'A burden shared, my dear,' she said, 'is something spared. The proverb says so, and I believe it's true. You surely wouldn't think now, father,' she continued, making use of the appellation most in favour with the sufferer, 'you surely wouldn't think that *I* could have a secret, or a care, and keep it from you. Why, James, suppose I meant it, sure I couldn't do it, for it would come out in spite of me, I know.'

'But, Ellen, supposing that long years ago,'—she listened with her heart upon her lips, as the old saying goes, for she perceived her words had moved him. 'Supposing that long years ago, before I ever knew you, dear, I had got into some trouble, some scrape, a boyish fault, perhaps, but still a fault that—'

and his tones grew still more serious—'had weighed upon my life as chains upon a convict's limbs, and blighted all my days.'

'Not all, poor boy!' said Ellen, tenderly, and utterly forgetting in his weakness that more than half-a-century had passed above that time-worn head. 'Not all, poor boy! we have had some sunny days since we have lived together and, please God, there are still some more in store for us. And, James, dear,' she added, rather shyly, 'you must not think I preach to you, I who am so unworthy; but if you *would* lift up your thoughts to Heaven, and say a prayer, dear—just a few words to ask our God to comfort you—you would feel much better. And after that to open out your heart to me would be as nothing.'

He was still silent, but she saw his face was working with suppressed emotion.

'Poor dear!' she whispered, as she passed her hand across his rugged brow. 'Poor dear! what can I say to comfort you? Oh, that I had words to make you understand how full is God's forgiveness to the penitent! And, dear, have you forgotten the sweet words I used to say to you:—

"New mercies each returning day
Hover around us as we pray;
New perils past, new sins forgiven,
New thoughts of God, new hopes of Heaven."

Is there not happiness in the thought, my dear, that the Almighty sees not as men see, but that knowing how much we have been tempted, He is ever ready to forgive us all our sins?'

She was not an eloquent discourser, that simple-hearted, loving woman, and, Heaven knows, she would have been no wise discusser of the points of faith; nevertheless, guided by the unerring instinct of a loving heart, she spoke out to the purpose; and Grayton, who would in all human probability have been deaf to the arguments of a licensed preacher, yielded to her tender prayers, and made what is called, in most emphatic language, a clean breast of it.

He told his history to her from his earliest days: How he had been a wretched 'prentice boy, starving on the scant food they gave him, and how, when urged on by the sight of generous fare, and of good things that stir in every way a boyish appetite, he had, in one most hated day, yielded himself to a great temptation, and become that shameless thing —a thief.

'From that time, Ellen, though perhaps you won't believe it,' said he, humbly, 'but from that time my life became a curse to me.'

'Hush, dear, it couldn't have been so, or you couldn't ever have been the good, kind husband that I've known you.'

'It was you that saved me, Ellen, for, five years ago—and that's the time that we've been married, dear—I was as poor a wretched creature as ever dared not call his soul his own. I used to go about quite moping like. I wasn't altogether bad, but I seemed like what the Scriptures tell us is being given over to a reprobate mind. I was not quite lost, but I was near upon it—yes, my precious, I was near upon it,—but you took me by the hand and saved me!'

And so he told her everything. He did not hide from her one single act of sin or cowardice, and verily, when all was said, the man found, in the consolation of that entire confidence, an exceeding great reward.

But for the poor trusting wife—for her whose pride had lain, more than aught else, in Grayton's rectitude—there was much inward shame and sorrow. To him she had looked up as to an example of all that a good friend and neighbour should be, and the treasure of his good name was one that his children's children—so she hoped—might live to honour. It was no light and trifling matter, then, to the sorrowing wife, to hear that Grayton's days had been darkened by the shadows of his former guilt, and that even now, in the autumn of his life, he trembled at the thought that another, and that one almost an enemy, was a sharer in his guilty secret.

She did not breathe a word of all this grief to Grayton, but only, when he ceased to speak, touched on the excuses that could be made for him, and on the extenuating circumstances of his youth and his privations.

'But, James,' the truthful woman urged, when the question of her husband's youthful errors gave place after awhile to a still more serious discussion on the subject of the missing paper—'James, what you say about that lawyer's—Mr. Cawthorne's doings, makes *him* look very black. He must have wanted to get money, surely, from the old Lord that drove the bargain.'

'Of course he did—a child might see his game.'

'And he was taken suddenly away, you say, before he'd lived out half his days? Ah, well! such things are never known to prosper. And so you got the paper, and Mr. Thomson know'd of it?'

'He did—bad luck to him. He knew I got it, and he's been hankering after it ever since that day. But, for all his threatenings, I wouldn't give it up—no, no, I wouldn't give it up.'

'But it was Yussy's, dear, not yours—or it was Mrs. Driver's. Oh, deary me! to think that poor lost woman—no, not lost, thank God! But just to think that Carry might be—what, James? What could the poor thing be called the day she got her rights?'

'Nothing much better than she is, my dear. She'd just be Mrs. Harley, and a great lady, as the world would think her.'

'And the boy?'

'Would be an Earl—a fine, rich, noble earl, with lands and castles, and a vote to rule the country. That's what he'd be, my dear, and then he'd be a nobleman at once—and grand and goodly, too, to look at, with a character for every virtue, and all the ladies kneeling at his feet.'

Ellen was, as may be supposed, in anything but a cheerful frame of mind; for her husband's troubles, past, present, and to come, oppressed her sorely; but, notwithstanding these antagonistic circumstances, a sense of the ludicrous overpowered her, and she could not restrain a laugh at the idea of Amelius Driver in the position described with such curt acrimony by her husband.

'To think of Yussy in fine clothes, and living with grand people! To think of such an ugly dwarf as that—' but here Mrs. Grayton checked herself, for she justly thought it was unchristianlike to make contemptuous mention, at that or any other moment, of the lad's personal deficiencies. The consideration, however, of Grayton's *quondam* pupil's disqualifications for a high estate led her thoughts back to the recent depredation which, in her opinion, he had certainly committed.

'It was he as did it, Grayton, and of that I'm just as sure as that I sit here this day.'

'But what reason have you for thinking

so, my dear? What in the name of wonder has put such a foolish thought into your head, when you must know as well as I do that the desk has never been away from us, and that the keys—'

'Has always been upon your watch-chain, James—I know that well. But yesterday, when I was out with little Nell—think well about it, dear—what was you doing all the while? and where,' she added, impressively, 'where had you put the keys?'

It was a suggestive question for the self-conceited man, who well remembered the luxurious slumber in which he had indulged, the while the cunning lad sat by him at his lesson; but like many another bolder culprit, Grayton found it easier to confess an error than a weakness, and for a moment he hesitated to avow that, by his own yielding to temptation, he had delivered himself bound into the hands of the enemy.

Ellen saw the truth at once, and spared him further trouble by saying abruptly,—

'You went to sleep, my dear. I know you did. It was very natural. And Yussy, the ungrateful boy; but, ah! that was quite natural, too—he took the keys, and found what was his own! I see it all before me now as plain as plain can be. I see the reason why he looked so pale, and trembled so, although I took but little heed of him just then; and—. Well, Grayton, dear—it's may be for the best, only, of course, there's something more to do, for Yussy didn't do this thing of his own head,' she added, shrewdly; 'and Mr. Thomson, maybe, will be coming here—or p'r'aps the lawyers, who can say?'

'The lawyers—curse them,' shouted Grayton; but Ellen laid her hand upon his lips. 'My dear—I didn't mean it,' he continued, meekly, 'only, you see this worry and the pain have shaken me a bit. Yes; I can see it all! It's Yussy has the paper, and all that's left for me is to have it all out with *him*. We mustn't lose a moment, dear. No; not a single moment, but away at once to town, and fetch the little rascal here.'

'But who away, dear, James? Sure you're not fit to go, a-shaking that way.'

'Me go, my precious! I shall never *go* again. My days, aye, perhaps my very hours, are numbered, Ellen, and I have heavy work to do before I go.'

She turned quite cold and livid as he spoke. So white indeed she was, that Grayton, looking in her face, feared he had said too much.

He drew her forehead down towards his lips, and whispered, as he kissed her,—

'Ellen—my faithful wife—my poor, dear woman—this is a sore, sore trial; but, as you have said to me a score of times, God knoweth what is best for us, and we must take the evil with the good.'

She was crying now—crying very bitterly, but still the tears relieved her, and she sobbed out bravely, 'I know it, James. I know it's very good for us to suffer; and yet

—it's easy saying when the time's far off; but when it really comes! But dear,' she whispered in a calmer voice, for Hope had flashed across her darkened mind one of its own electric lights — 'but, dear, I cannot see why you should be so timersome. You've been as sick as this a score of times, and never lost your heart before.'

'Didn't I,' responded Jemmy, wearily, 'well, I'm a coward, that is all. But, Ellen, be that as it may, I *must* make up my last accounts before the sun goes down. I must see Carry Driver, precious, and her son; I must see justice done at last, and try to make my peace with Heaven.'

She had ceased to remonstrate with him, indeed, she could but feel that what he had to do had best be undertaken quickly.

'My dear,' he continued, after a pause, during which Ellen, whose every sense had grown painfully acute, noticed that his respiration had grown more difficult, and his speech less clear. 'Ellen, my love, you must take a journey for me to-day. Nay, not a long one. Only to London — only to Short's Gardens, and bring those two together back with you.'

'Me take a journey, Grayton!' she exclaimed. 'Me leave you in the state you're in! You couldn't think it, James. Oh, no; you couldn't think it,' and with an imploring gesture, she raised his hand and pressed it to her lips. He could not but be touched by her great care and never-ceasing tenderness; but yet he swerved not from his purpose, and never heeding her objections, he gave her his directions for the journey.

'You will take the earliest train,' he said, 'and not delay a moment. Don't try to walk, you'd never find your road; besides, the time's too precious. You must take a cab and drive to No. 8, Short's Gardens,—don't forget—and say to Mrs. Driver that I'm a dying man and want to see her.'

She dried her eyes and never said another word, but took the child and gave it to a neighbour's care, — a neighbour whom she trusted, and who promised to look in from time to time on James, and see he lacked for nothing.

The journey was a very short one, yet it seemed long to Ellen. Aye, long indeed, for, all the while, although she told herself her fears were vain, an inward voice that would not be gainsaid kept ever murmuring in her husband's words, 'His days are numbered.'

She arrived at Short's Gardens at last! but only to find that half, at least, of the sick man's mission must be unfulfilled, for Mrs. Driver, so the neighbours told her, had 'gone out to walk,' and Yussy's toilet was not yet completed.

CHAPTER XIV.

YUSSY STUDIES FASHIONS TO ADORN HIS BODY.

MASTER DRIVER had left his bed unusually early on the morning of Mrs. Grayton's visit. It was the custom of that pleasure-loving young gentleman to linger long between the sheets and blankets (his couch was far more warmly covered than his mother's), and waiting till the fire burned up, and the hot buttered toast was ready for him, to while away the passing hour with golden dreams of a most gorgeous future. But on this occasion—it was a rare occurrence—Yussy and his much enduring parent had had, what the former irreverently called a 'rumpus.' The word, whatever may be its origin, was scarcely an appropriate one, for it had been an extremely one-sided affair, as Mrs. Driver, almost immediately after the commencement of the combat, had drawn off her forces in a manner more pusillanimous than dignified. Yussy remained, therefore, decidedly master of the field, for his mother, in furtherance of a project of her own, and moved thereto by some vaunting, but not altogether comprehensible expressions to which Yussy had in the heat of discussion given utterance, had left her home betimes, and betaken herself for a very doubtful kind of consolation to Mr. Andrew Thomson, at his residence in James Street.

Yussey's hands were full of business, when the cab, conveying sorrowing Mrs. Grayton stopped at that humble door. He was standing before a broken mirror which hung against the wall—standing in his short corduroy trousers, and with his straight, long hair brushed up with care from his low, cunning forehead. Upon the bed, and close beside him, was a new suit; a blue frock coat—he would look well in that—a dandy primrose waistcoat, and the *rest* in showy chocolate-brown. Very tenderly, and with eyes of conscious pride did Master Driver look upon his new possessions. How long it was since he had first coveted a dress like that! How long it was since that eventful Sunday when he had watched the smart apprentices, the titmice of the London shops, dressed bravely in their broadcloth, and each one looking, so the poor boy thought, a gentleman every inch of him! At that time Yussy looked and longed, but no hope cheered him onward to endeavour— but now —ah, happy youth! the desire of thy heart is given thee, and thou canst step forth in thy '*braverie*,' a mark for admiration and for envy!

So absorbed was Mr. Driver in the contemplation of his own distinguished person, that Ellen had knocked twice at the door before he became aware of her near neighbourhood, and then he answered in that peculiar voice, half boy's, half man's, which is not, strictly speaking, musical, that whoever knocked had better not be making such a jolly row, for he was busy.

'But, Yussy,' remonstrated Ellen, venturing to open the door just a quarter of an inch that he might hear her voice the better, 'I have come on urgent business — business from Mr. Grayton. He's very ill to-day, and hopes you'll come at once to see him.'

'He be hanged,' responded Amelius, who was engaged in fastening round his throat a narrow neckcloth, black, with scarlet stripes.

'No, don't say that; he's very ill, and thinks he's going to die. He wants to see your mother too, but the people down below say she is not at home.'

'No more she is; gone out upon a spree. I say,' continued Yussy, opening the door just wide enough to show his ugly face—'I say, what's up down there?' And he pointed over his shoulder, with an idea probably that he thereby indicated the direction of Grayton's cottage.

There was but little time for explanation or for discussion on the events which had occurred in the small suburban dwelling, for every minute was precious to Ellen Grayton, and therefore, as the surest, and indeed the only way of inducing Yussy to obey her husband's behests, she decided, rather too hastily, perhaps, on divulging what had occurred, and the more than suspicions that both she and Grayton entertained that he, Yussy, was not guiltless in the matter.

'You see I wasn't told to say it to you, Yussy,' she began, 'but only, do you know, I'm sure there's some excuse. You couldn't see your mother wronged, and so you took the marriage lines to give to her.'

'Who told you that I took anythink?' asked Yussy, who had grown red and pale alternately. 'And if I did, it was my own, and I'd a right to it. And don't you think it was for her, because it warn't. Why, I know all about it, now. I know she sold me —so she did—for money that she spent, and kept me out of all my rights. Ugh! There's a pretty mother for you.'

Ellen, who had very high and proper ideas of the reverence due to the parental character, was intensely shocked at Yussy's tone of defiance and disrespect, and showed her displeasure to him plainly.

'Yussy, this is not right,' she said; 'and you can never know what drove your mother to that course. It is not for us to judge,' she said more gently, and recollecting doubtless that it was by persuasion rather than by anger that Master Yussy was most likely to be influenced—'no, it is not for us to judge; and she must be very sorry now, as Grayton is, I'm sure. Not that *he* wronged you, don't you think it, for he was only waiting till you was wiser like, and older, to—to—to tell you all he'd done.'

'Oh! I dare say; that's a likely story,' said Yussy, with a sneer, 'but howsomever, if he's likely to speak up I'll come along with you. Just you wait outside a bit, while I rig up.' And so saying, Amelius closed the door upon his visitor, and continued the agreeable occupation of making himself look like a gentleman. And, verily, it might be said that he had studied the art to some purpose; as was apparent when he emerged from the privacy of his chamber, and stood in the full light of day before the astonished eyes of the unsophisticated Mrs. Grayton.

'Law, Yussy!' she said, 'sure you're not a-going out in that figure?'

She might well ask the question, for certainly he was a startling object as he stood there in his pride before her. The coat—a Moses' one—not made for his peculiar figure, but hanging loose about his poor, thin pigeon-breast, and tightly stretched across the slight protuberance—it could be scarcely called a hump—which rose above one graceless shoulder-blade. And then the hat, so large and new and glossy, with the gay, gorgeous neck-tie, and the great gilt chain and pin; were unwonted sights to see in that dull place, and neighbours' heads were thrust outside their doors to look and laugh at Yussy in his new 'turn-out.' He did not condescend to answer Ellen's question, but with conscious dignity stepped before her into the waiting vehicle, and told her, energetically, to 'come on.'

'I'd something else to do to-day than walk off there to see old Jemmy,' said he, crossly, as Ellen, infinitely disgusted by his rudeness and flippancy, took her place opposite. 'I'd got to see a lovely gal—no, not a gal exactly, but a nice fancy woman—who'll cry her pretty eyes out when she finds I've "hooked it."'

'Law, Yussy! and you a child—to talk that way?'

'A child! I like that. No one knows my age—in course not! A poor love-child—so they called me. Never had a father?—oh, no, not at all! But I know better, and I've been to see the register. You wouldn't think it, now, but I shall be sixteen in May.'

'Sixteen! Why, then, you're getting on

to be a man, of course,' said Ellen, who felt it necessary to say something, but whose attention was absorbed by the contemplation of that wizen, mischievous face, which looked, indeed, as if frail 'nature had been corrupted with some bribe' to make men turn from it with loathing. She had, as we have seen, a very kindly heart—so kindly, that the sentiment of pity for the great misfortune of his ugliness stole over her, as Yussy, in his boyish vanity, declared himself a man; and feeling how debarred he was, and ever must be, from the quiet joys which made her home a happy one, she said with almost tenderness,—

'My dear, I hope you'll turn your thoughts to many better things if you grow rich and great, as Grayton says you will. Of course you'll see to make your mother comfortable in a nice country cottage—that would suit her best. She'd get quite strong and hearty in the country, and then—'

'I wish you wouldn't jabber so, and go on

that way about mother. I've heard enough about her goings on, I tell you! Why, when I was a little fellow they used to jeer me in the streets about her, and almost made me mad at first; but then I thought—Lord! what is she to me? She took and cut away, and took the money, too, be hanged to her!'

'Oh, Yussy!' exclaimed Ellen, greatly shocked. 'Oh, Yussy, don't talk so dreadful!'

'It isn't dreadful, it's the truth; but I was a long time coming to it, Mrs. Grayton. I was a little chap when mother left me—not six years old, I reckon—but I was very fond of her, I know. I used to lie awake at nights and cry for her long after she went away; and after that the first thing I remember was the fellows chaffing me about her, and—ah, well! it isn't any use a'going on; but p'r'aps if mother had been better—'

He stopped abruptly, and Ellen, who did not like to seem to watch him, fancied she saw him pass his hand across his eyes. They did not speak again, but rattled onwards to the station, whence a third-class carriage soon conveyed him to the sad, silent house where Jemmy Grayton had for some hours, in almost uncontrollable impatience, waited for their coming.

CHAPTER XV.

AN HOUR TOO LATE.

To the observant reader it has probably become apparent that Master Driver, taking into consideration the high position which he expected at some future time to fill, had seen the necessity of remodelling his tone of conversation, and of attending seriously to his parts of speech. That the amount of rubbing up which he had been enabled to bestow upon his manners and his turns of expression had not been productive of much outward polish it is impossible to deny; but according to his own ideas Yussy was progressing rapidly in outward accomplishments, and accumulating for their future exhibition to an admiring world all the 'good gifts that grace a gentleman.'

Grayton was still lying on his bed, even as she had left him, dressed, and outside the patchwork coverlid (the fruits of Ellen's labours), when his wife came softly to his side and drew the curtain back. He had not heard their steps within the passage, for he was sleeping heavily. Yet not exactly sleeping—it was a stupor rather—though Ellen, whose disposition was, as we have seen, a sanguine one, looked at his passive face with pleasure, and thought — poor soul — that 'James was on the way to mend.'

He had not lain so many minutes. In truth, his mind was working far too quickly for the body's rest; and long before his wife was able to decide whether it were better to awake him gently from his slumber, the sick man's eyes half opened, with that strangely puzzled look which eyes will wear on an awakening from a troubled sleep.

'It was his right,' he muttered; 'and may God forgive me—both for *their* sins and my own!'

Ellen laid her cool hand softly on his burning forehead.

'My dear,' she said, 'I've come at last, and brought him.'

'Brought who? Oh, Ellen, I've had such a dream. Don't leave me, dear, again—I wouldn't die alone. I grew so frightened when the house was still. I thought of flames and judgment, and of—. Oh! my God, to think we *must* die, alone. Alone—alone—yes, all alone!' he went on, murmuring, whilst Ellen, who was wholly unprepared to find him in a state of mind so wandering and so strange, stood looking at his frightened face in mute dismay. But after a few moments he recovered in some degree both his memory and his composure, and his thoughts reverting to the cause for his wife's sudden journey, he said, with a calmness which lulled for the moment Ellen's fears to sleep,—

'My dear—I'm very troublesome and foolish—I dwelt too much, perhaps, upon this business before I went to sleep. You see, the secret has been lying on my mind for years—and it gives a kind of shock, you know, when such a weight is taken off. I don't know either that I'm quite the thing—I've got a pain—the old pain in my heart;' and he breathed a low suffocating sigh which frightened Ellen sorely.

'I'll send for Doctor Collins,' she said, hastily.

'No, don't—I'd rather see the boy. I *must* see Melius—I couldn't die without. He shouldn't curse me in my grave!—no, no,—he shouldn't!' And so excited did he become, that the bed, aye the very room, seemed to shake beneath his agitated frame.

'Don't—don't, my dear,' cried Ellen, at her wit's end with fear. 'I'll bring him—hush—be quiet. Think of Nelly!—think of Heaven!—think of—. Oh, God, take pity on him!' and in her wild despair she fell upon her knees, and cried to God to comfort the despairing sinner.

It was a fearful crisis, and an awful change

took place in Grayton's face ere it was over; but he rallied for awhile, and spoke again collectedly.

'I'm worse a deal, I fear, than you believe, my precious!' so he said, in a weak voice that went to Ellen's heart. 'Don't you cry now, dear—you've got the child—where is she, Ellen, love? I'd like to see her blessed face again!—and bring the boy up here—poor fellow—it may do him good; he's got into bad ways, I fear, and may be it's my fault. Oh, Ellen, dear—my good and patient wife, remember this—it will be a comfort to you in your dying hours—that through the years we've spent together it's you has taught me to look up to Heaven, and made the valley lighter to me. Bring him up now, my dear—bring him to say that he forgives me! I wouldn't die with that boy's curse upon my head.'

She flew downstairs—never in all her life had Ellen's steps been quicker—she flew downstairs, and calling out in haste to Yussy, bade him go up at once.

'You'll find him on the bed,' she said; 'and go up gently, dear. He's near his end,' —her voice was almost choked by sobs— 'he's near his end. Don't *you* be rough with him. If he has sinned, he's in the hands of God to punish him. Don't you go on to let him see that you—'

She could not finish her entreaty for the great gush of tears that choked her utterance; and then, tying on her cloak with trembling fingers, she went forth with all the speed she could to bring the doctor to her husband's side.

An hour elapsed, and Ellen sat beside the kitchen fire, with little Nelly sleeping on her knee, waiting for Yussy's step upon the creaking stairs. He did not come. What could it mean? They had had more than time, she thought, to speak out all their minds; and Grayton was so weak—poor man!—so very weak, that such a long discourse might weary him. She had grown very nervous—her fingers cold and stiff, for in her all-absorbing fears she had been forgetful of the fire, which had burned low within the grate. So, wrapping Nelly up in her warm cloak, she crept on to the window, and looking out, watched for the doctor's coming.

It was not long delayed, and then—still with her daughter in her arms—Ellen went up the stairs before him, waiting one moment at the door to listen.

She heard but these few words—words said by Yussy in an eager, hurried voice,—

'Then it wasn't you? You didn't drive her to it? You didn't help her take the old brute's money, and then hide up the proofs?'

'Never, so help me God!' said Grayton, solemnly. 'I came into his papers—Cawthorne's papers—when he died, and that was after she—after your mother went away. There are more proofs, my boy, if they are wanting — letters of Cawthorne's, which you'll find in the old desk. And now shake hands—my breath comes very short—shake hands, my boy, and say we're parting friends!'

Yussy placed his small, puny palm, all warm with life, into the broad, clammy hand that feebly stretched towards him. His voice was rather husky as he said Good-by, and muttered that he had nothing to forgive.

'And so,' he added, 'you keep up your heart. You're not a going to die this time —you're only low. I'll send the missus up;' and glad to leave a painful scene, Yussy approached the door.

'Go in,' he said, on seeing Mrs. Grayton's tearful face, 'go in. I think he's rather better, and I didn't worrit him, but told him not to fret himself along of me.'

He hastened down the stairs, and Ellen might, if she had been in the mood to watch his movements, have heard the street door closed behind him, and seen his showy, stumpy figure, as it quickly passed on through the garden gate.

The Doctor followed upon Ellen's footsteps wonderingly, for he too had heard the last few words, the meaning of which was as a sealed book to him.

He felt the patient's pulse, and looked into his restless eyes.

'You cannot bear the light?' he asked.

'Not well,' moaned Grayton, feebly; 'but it isn't there I feel the most. It's in the heart, Doctor, it's in the heart.'

'I know it, my poor man. Keep quiet. I will send you something;' and he went downstairs with Ellen.

She watched him as he put on his great coat deliberately, and hoped—oh! how she hoped—that he would speak, and say that James was not so very ill. His face was extremely grave. That frightened her, and with a desperate wish to know the truth, she said, almost before she knew the words were uttered,—

'Doctor—please tell me—will he die?'

He was a tender-hearted man, and held

his hand out to her in silence. It was enough. She did not speak, but pressing the sleeping child still closer to her bosom, she went, with a dull pain at her own heart, upstairs.

She laid the child down close to him, so that his hand could touch it, and sitting down quite near the bed, she laid her cheek to his.

'Ellen, my love,' he feebly said, 'don't leave me any more. I've made my peace, I trust, with man, and prayed to be forgiven. It is evening now, I know,—time for the hymn. Say it all through, my dear, and learn it, love, to little Nell when I am in my grave.'

It was a hard task—so hard that, only for her great love, her courage would have failed her; but she went bravely through it, verse by verse. It was a prayer almost throughout—a fervent, spirit-stirring prayer; and as each humble cry for pardon and support fell on the dying ear, a slumber—so it seemed to Ellen—peaceful as a sinless child's, stole over his poor, changed face:—

'Abide with me from morn to eve,
For without thee I cannot live;
Abide with me when night is nigh,
For without thee I dare not die.'

She gradually lowered her voice to a whisper as she repeated the closing lines, and then, seeing that he lay quite still, she took the child (who now showed, by a restless movement, that she was about to cause some disturbance in the darkened chamber) within her arms, and softly stole from the room.

There was a neighbour in the kitchen—one of those kindly gossips who seem ubiquitous where death and sickness reign. She came, she said, to see if she could sit up with Grayton—help her to do her work—help her to bear her grief. Alas! poor soul, she knew in this her sorest hour, how vain is human sympathy, and that worthy Mrs. Mason, with her fresh glowing face, was no more able to minister to her sorrowing spirit, than would have been the 'tenderest heart' most near her own, who, as the poet says, is ignorant of—

'Half the reasons why we smile or sigh.'

'If you will only take poor baby, Mrs. Mason,' Ellen said, 'you'll help me more than anything. I dare not leave him—not a moment. Thank you, so very much!' and laying little Nelly on the matron's ample lap, she was returning to her post, when a loud, sharp voice within the passage made her stop in fear.

'I say, where's that young varmint, Meelius Driver? Gad! if I catch hold of him, I'll—'

The voice was Andrew Thomson's. There was no mistaking it; and Ellen, in her dread that it should awaken Grayton, laid hold upon his arm with little ceremony, and drew him forward to the kitchen.

'Don't speak so loud,' she whispered, 'or you will disturb him. He's very ill upstairs. The doctor thinks he won't recover.'

'Who? Yussy? Don't you flam me. I

know better. He was as well as you or I an hour ago. But he's been at his old thieving tricks again; and I'll be hanged if I'm not quits with him.'

'What has he taken? Answer quick, I haven't got a moment—'

'Taken? Why robbed that fool old Grayton's desk, and blabbed about it to his mother, d—n her. I say, what's Jemmy up to? I must have a word with him, I tell you.'

'You cannot,' answered Ellen passionately, for she was worked up by the presence of that evil man into a state of excitement most unusual to her. 'You cannot. I have told you he is dying, and you shall not, must not, see him.'

'Not see him—that's a good 'un. It's a lie of yours to keep him close; and what's more, it's my belief he sold the paper, and you know it.'

'The paper wasn't his to sell,' said Ellen; 'it was Amelius Driver's, and he has got his own at last.'

'Curse him to —,' cried Thomson furiously, and before Ellen was able to resist him he was up the stairs and stood by Grayton's bed.

His hand was on the curtain as the frightened, trembling woman laid a grasp upon his arm to draw him back.

'Stay, let me speak,' she whispered; and then it was—'Father, there's some one here who wants you; some one that says—why, James, dear—speak! Father, what's this? Oh, Heaven! he's gone, and no one by his side to see him die!'

Yes, it was quite true that Jemmy Grayton's soul had passed away without a struggle in that heavy, dreamless slumber! No human eye had seen him breathe his last; but 'some one,' far more powerful than Andrew Thomson, had come for Jemmy—had 'wanted him,' as Ellen said, and would not be put off.

Thomson, having convinced himself that the poor widow's fears had not deceived her, did not tarry long within the house of mourning. He did a stroke of business though before he went, by hunting in every likely and unlikely place for the important desk which had contained the treasure that he coveted. He searched, but searched in vain; and after half-an-hour thus unprofitably spent, he came to the highly unsatisfactory conclusion that Master Driver had not done his work by halves, and that to circumvent that young gentleman's plans would be a work of greater difficulty than he had at first imagined.

CHAPTER XVI.

SUSAN TAKES HERSELF TO TASK.

THE course of our story now takes us once more into the precincts of Cousin Chrissy's prison, where a piece of most unexpected intelligence has at last succeeded in throwing a ray of sunshine into that shady place. It was Susan who was the pleased announcer of that glad event, and the two women wept tears of joy on either side the iron-clad door as they talked over the details which the kind girl had brought with her.

'It is such happy news,' said Mrs. Fletcher, 'that I can scarce believe it! To think that she—our own dear Margery—should be restored to health and reason, should know us all again, and be my own dear child once more, is too much happiness!' And Cousin

Chrissy, in her exceeding joy at the probable restoration to society of one whom she had learnt to look upon as morally dead, forgot for the moment her own perilous situation, and the clouds which lowered above her head.

'God has indeed been merciful,' said Susan reverently, 'and just, as well as merciful; for they say, dear Cousin Chrissy, that that evil being, the man whose cruel conduct destroyed the feeble balance of poor Margaret's brain, is a sad sufferer now, and that the very shock which by the Almighty's mercy may work *her* cure, has crushed *him* so that his very life's in danger.'

They remained for the rest of the period allowed for Susan's visit in anxious conversation on the probable means that would be taken for the perfecting of Margaret's cure; for the young girl—the same that Clavering spoke of as a raving maniac in the inn at Lille—was very dear to Cousin Chrissy's heart. It was for her sake, and for the part she felt that she had borne in the poor child's misfotrune, that Mrs. Fletcher shed the bitterest tears in her first hour of trial; and it was on Margery's account that now the well-springs of pure joy gushed from her gladdened eyes.

Susan left the prison on that morning with a lighter heart than she had known for weeks; but long before she reached her lonely home, the one bright ray had faded from the picture and left it all in gloom.

The greatest aggravation to Susan's trials at this period of her life arose from the conflicting duties that she saw before her. Already in her life had she severely felt how dangerous a thing it is sometimes for the head to listen to the heart's suggestions, and for the judgment to be swayed by the affections. She was not a common character, that young solitary girl, and moreover she had learned in the hard school of adversity to throw aside all thoughts of self, and—casting her bread upon the waters—to hope that after many days it would be found again by her who had trusted to the faithful promises.

But with all her excellent training, and despite the uncompromising severity with which she judged her faults, and performed mental penance even for her weaknesses, Susan had still to fight sometimes hard battles with herself—battles, too, in which she did not always come off victorious.

The deep and soul-searching investigations to which she had been wont to subject herself, had early revealed to her the disagreeable truth that the chief of her besetting sins was jealousy. She never remembered the time when the craving for exclusive affection from those she loved had not embittered the enjoyment she felt in their regard. *Le mieux* was decidedly in Susan's case *l'ennemi du bien*; and if this were so in her earlier and her childish days, how much the greater was the evil when a woman's ripened thoughts and feelings were craving to be satisfied? To those who have followed with any degree of interest the description of Susan Brigham's character and career, it will be evident that the ruined merchant's daughter was not without a share of pride, which, in more instances than one, had stood in the way of her own happiness; for it was by the promptings of pride that she had been induced (when a young and blooming girl, whose beauty and whose grace could well supply the place of birth and fortune) to hide her gracious gifts beneath a cold exterior, so that scarcely one who knew her but was in utter ignorance of the warmth—the almost passionate warmth of feeling—which lay hidden in her heart, like the electric fluid in the solid mass of earthly material.

An early disappointment (to use the technical term in use when speaking of blighted love affairs) had certainly been instrumental in the apparently hermetical sealing-up of poor Susan's heart against the natural affections of her age and sex. She was very young when she first became an inmate of her godmother's quiet country house in Devonshire. She had known sorrow, too, of late, for she had left a suddenly impoverished home, in which there never more could meet together the attached and lately prosperous family, whose riches did indeed seem literally to have taken themselves wings and flown away, so unexpectedly had their distress come upon them.

Susan then, when she arrived at Lee Grange, was in the mood to seek for love and comfort. Hers was a feeling and, though none might deem it so from any outward signs, an excitable nature; and there was one in that dull, quiet place, who was, unhappily for her, the likeliest man and in the likeliest position to call forth all her latent sympathies.

A widower, still in the prime of life, handsome and attractive in person, and *left* with one little lovely girl to add to the interest of his situation, was exactly the individual to occupy the vacant place in such a heart as

Susan's. It was a very lonely place, as I have said, where Cousin Chrissy lived, and neighbours were both few and far between, so that it was natural for the girl to dwell in fancy on the one kind, social friend who shed, what was to her a happy brightness on their quiet home. But Clayton Bernard —for he it was who all unconsciously had taken this large part in Susan Brigham's life —had not, as far as men, and even women could see, any present thought of giving to his little girl another mother. And then the life he led in that secluded village was so utterly unexciting, that with a calm and equal mind he went forth to his daily duties as a parish priest, and gave no thought to love or passion.

Verily it is a truth to ponder on, that 'the sight of means to do ill deeds, make ill deeds done.' And if this be the case (which I think no one will venture to deny), is not the converse also true, that in the absence of such dangerous means, and the still more valuable absence of the excitement which accompanies sometimes the contemplation of our neighbours' vices, lies our best chance of safety?

Clayton Bernard could not be said to enjoy the blessing of a cold temperament; on the contrary, under propitious circumstances he would, in all probability, have been quite ready (seeing that though he had deeply mourned his wife, his heart was not buried in her grave) to fall in love when called upon to do so; but with all his readiness for such an event, it must be owned that, despite her youth and prettiness, Susan Brigham, with her placid *retenue* of manners and her maidenly reserve, was scarcely one to awaken in the widower's breast feelings responsive to her own. He saw, and he admired her,—admired her for her feminine gentleness, her constant and untiring attention to her duties, and for the total absence of vanity and affectation which was remarkable in all she said and did. He used to praise her openly to

Miss Llewellen, for Mrs. Fletcher was an old maid then, but with a leaning to such pleasant confidences, and the good lady had a hope sometimes that 'dearest Susan' would in time become the Vicar's wife, and fill the place upon his hearth which death had long left vacant.

It was a pleasant dream, but not one fated to be realized, for ere long there lighted on that tranquil spot a radiant vision—a most fair coquette—a brilliant, showy girl, by whose obtrusive charms poor Susan's fainter beauty fell into shade at once!

There is no need to dwell on all that the weak child (for she was nothing more just then) went through at that most bitter period of her life. She had no right to feel so, you will say. She was a forward and precocious damsel, some will urge, to suffer for a man who had no thought of her, nor ever gave her cause to hope that she had touched his heart. All this is sadly true, perhaps, and yet poor Susan may lay some claim to pity, for 'human love is not the growth of human will,' and very young and very modest maidens (disbelieve it if you will) are often nearer giving up their hearts to men who treat them with indifference, than to the ardent lover 'sighing like furnace' by their side, and awakening often more of fear than tenderness.

Be this as it may, Miss Llewellen's quiet little god-daughter had some not over-happy hours to pass through at that momentous period of her life. I say 'momentous,' for it worked a great, and not entirely a wholesome change, in all her views of life, and all her hitherto bright joyous prospects for the future. She had no future now, she felt, at least none that could deserve the name, but only a dull passive bearing of the present, which brought, as every morning sun broke forth so bright for others, only an added weight of weariness for her.

Susan was little more than eighteen when this calamity befell her, and, as was reasonably to be expected, she soon, to a certain extent at least, recovered from it; but a change—complete and life-long—had come over the young girl's character during that painful process, *viz.* the awakening from the heart's delusions; and Susan rose up to her duties after that short, but sunny dream, an altered being. She did not hug her sorrow foolishly, but on the contrary, her very shame to think that she had loved unasked, caused her to chase away with angry vehemence the memory of her disappointment. But she grew older, colder, less impulsive from that hour, and contenting herself with a conscientious discharge of all that had been given her to do, she lived on, as I said, without that blessed pastime, Hope, to make the Present happy.

The great and overwhelming misfortunes which had so unexpectedly overtaken her benefactress, formed another turning-point in Susan Brigham's life, and changed again her character for the better. How hard to tread, her path was, at this period, none but herself and one sure, trusted friend could tell. But Susan went with courage on her way, and only faltered when (may she be forgiven for her human weakness!) the news rung out that Margaret Mayford's reason was restored to her.

An utter hatred for, and an intense disgust at, her own motives, crushed down Susan's never over-buoyant spirits, as, with her needle in her hand, she stitched her useful woman's work in solitude. Heavens! how she loathed herself for the mean, pitiful jealousy which stood between her and the joy she should have felt at Margaret's probable recovery. A thousand painful recollections came in crowds to swell the bitter current of her feelings—a thousand memories of the far greater love that Cousin Chrissy felt for Margaret, who was in truth the child of her affections, and her own near kinsman's child.

And what was *she* beside that stronger

love?—a nothing, a forgotten thing! The time of sorrow, and the mingling of their tears—the bitter cup which they had drunk together, and the sad dreary hours spent outside the prison walls—they would be all forgotten in the joy of Margaret's return, and in the soothing of her sweet caresses. For already Susan had in her own mind arrived at the conclusion that Maggie's restoration to reason would be permanent, and had allowed her imagination to dwell on the probability of Cousin Chrissy's acquittal, and her return to the tranquil Western home, which she had been unwise to quit for gayer scenes.

Do not despise this lonely and love-seeking girl, as in her isolation she broods upon her uncared-for future. We have all of us, would we but seek them out with earnestness, *some* dark and unswept corners in our hearts, where lurks the dust and dross which hides itself from our 'moat'-blinded eyes, and chokes the little good within us. So in Heaven's name, let us be merciful to our fellow-sinners, remembering that we—

> 'Are but children of a larger growth,
> Our appetites as apt to change as theirs,
> And full as craving too and full as vain.'

This child, then—this poor, weak, clinging daughter of our common mother—sat by her fire, striving to build her hope alone in Heaven, but carried away, in spite of all her efforts, by the smaller, lower passions that belong to earth.

The short winter twilight was closing round the solitary girl, and with a wearied, languid look, she was rising to prepare her evening meal, when the door softly opened, and a woman closely veiled advanced towards her.

She did not say a word, but, bursting into tears, held out her hands imploringly.

'I do not know you,' Susan was beginning. 'I think there must be some mistake. Won't you sit down?' and she drew a chair towards her unknown visitor.

'Rest! not till you have heard me—not till

I have told you who I am—not till you have seen my face.' And as she spoke, she threw up her concealing veil, and disclosed the pale, but strikingly-handsome features of Olive Bernard.

Susan had but a slight acquaintance with Gerald Bernard's wife, nor was she, any more than Marian Clavering, prejudiced in her favour.

To almost every thinking being there is something repulsive in the very fact of mystery; and that there was a veil of that unsatisfactory material wrapped about the handsome Olive was beyond a question. And then her manners and her habits, especially to one retiring and unobtrusive as was Susan Brigham, were decidedly against her in that young lady's estimation. What wonder, then, that the quick-witted and observant Olive perceived at once that there was no cordial welcome for her beneath that lowly roof.

Had she been one whit less suffering,

tired, and crushed down, she would have turned to go at once; but bodily illness had within a few short hours combined with other causes to repress all pride and every angry passion in Olive Bernard's breast. So, sitting down, with a wild, wailing cry she flung her arms upon the table, scattering poor Susan's working materials ruthlessly, and rocked herself to and fro in anguish unmistakable.

It was not in Susan's nature to witness any suffering and give no sign of pity; so she spoke soothing words to the dejected creature who, when the first violence of her emotion had passed away, said in a broken voice—

'You will turn me away, of course,—you will not be the first of *his* people—his friends who will have done so; but I thought I would try once more—once more before I went to—to my father, Susan—let me call you so!' and she looked up beseechingly in the young girl's face.

Susan was touched by the gentleness of one who had hitherto been so little remarkable for the display of any of the softer qualities, and she hastened to assure her visitor that, as far as her most limited means of affording hospitality would allow, Olive should not want the shelter of a home.

'But I am very poor,' she added; 'so poor that I am glad to work, both to chase thought away and find the means of living. You did not know of this, perhaps—nor that I have but this one room to live in?'

'Indeed I did not, but I should have come the same if the one room were smaller, poorer still. I want so much to have a friend—a friend that's good and true—a friend that would not leave me were I sick and ill, and who would speak a word for me to Gerald.'

There was a tone of such plaintive dependence and entreaty in Olive's words, that Susan's heart quite warmed towards her. And then, was she not *his* brother's wife—*his* sister, whose earthly fate she felt, so often and with such bitter pangs, was in *her* hands to soften or to blight for ever?

She drew her nearer to the scanty fire, and bade her welcome to the best she had.

'It won't be much,' she added, cheerily, 'but we must eke it out, and—'

'You surely do not think I am a pauper,' interrupted Olive, with something that savoured greatly of her old, rather underbred impetuosity. 'I didn't come to sponge upon you, that isn't in my line; but I have such a weight upon my heart; and then that odious man, that Redfern!—'

'Heavens!' Susan said. 'Why, he's your father.'

There was a triumphant smile on Olive's face, for truly she was mean enough (she had been so badly trained) to feel a pride in her left-handed blood-relationship to the old worldly Earl. Yes, there was a real smile of satisfaction on her face when she and Olive, seated at that unpretending tea-table, discoursed on the same subjects which had so lately called the blush of shame to Marian Clavering's brow.

They talked long into the silent night, and Olive opened what she called her heart to her new friend. But did she tell her *all* during that long confession? I can only ask who does? Does the spendthrift with his list of debts, which a kind father has agreed to pay, ever write down the whole of them? Never; he keeps some in reserve, whether from lingering shame at their amount, or from a wish—a common one—to seem a trifle better than he is. And so it was that Olive, in the presence of that pure, true-hearted girl, found it impossible (it had been an easy task in Marian's drawing-room) to tell the unvarnished tale of all her mother's errors and her own base deceptions. She could not say to Susan—there, in cold blood, and with those clear, sweet eyes upon her—that she, her guest and now admitted friend, had borne another appellation, and was, in fact, the Isabel Forbes at mention of whose name a cry of horror throughout the length and breadth of England had, some few years before, rung out so loudly. She showed a prudent reticence in keeping back such facts as these, for it may be doubted whether Susan, with all her enlarged benevolence and quiet Christian charity, would have been quite pleased to share her couch, as now she did, with the repentant Olive, whose prayers before she went to bed were—although poor Susan guessed it not—more a propitiatory offering for the gaining of *her* good opinion than a humble entreaty for pardon and protection at the throne of grace.

CHAPTER XVII.

FLORENCE BERNARD ACTS UPON IMPULSE.

'CLAYTON, I am growing awfully tired of this stupid place,' said Florence Bernard to her husband, as she lay panting under her mosquito-net, and waiting for the fresh sea evening breeze to blow upon her languid frame.

They had left Madeira, for Florence had soon wearied of the monotony of that lovely sanatorium, and were now cruising amongst the West India Islands in a yacht which a friend of Bernard's (a rich man, who like themselves was killing time and cheating care in the tropics) had placed at their disposal. They were on shore at Port Royal when Florence, whose spirits had considerably revived during her two months' absence from England, broke out into the above expression of discontent; and, as usual, her slightest wish was a law to her husband.

'My darling,' he responded, 'I will go anywhere with you, and so, I am sure, will Gerald. He won't hear of being called an invalid, and as for you—'

'Oh! I am strong enough for anything; I have quite got over that stupid, nervous illness. Nervous, indeed! Florence Harley suffering from such a stupid complaint as that! I'm quite ashamed to think of it.'

Captain Bernard, who was lying lazily on a cane-bottomed sofa, drinking sangaree, looked with some surprise at his pretty sister-in-law, whose newly-found vivacity, coupled as it was with the warning letters he had again received from Ernest, was an enigma which he found it difficult to solve.'

'You are a very capricious young woman, Flo, I fear,' was his half-playful comment on her words, 'and I half begin to think that it is nothing more than love of contradiction which makes you cry out so for change.'

'And always when the mail's expected!' put in her husband, innocently, and little reckoning on the effect his words would have upon Flo's clear complexion, in which the crimson roses and the white followed each other in rapid succession after his imprudent speech.

'I hate letters,' she said, with a languor which looked like affectation after the lively tones in which she had so short a time before been speaking — 'I hate letters; they're always such a bore!—Mamma complaining of her poverty, and of Alick's meanness. Poor fellow, he would give anything he has! And then I can't endure his marriage to that odious, toadying London girl!'

'Anything more?' asked Clayton, looking up with a smile from a letter he was writing.

'Yes, a great deal more, for I cannot bear to see him gulled so. He's the best creature in the world, and won't imagine for a moment why they have insisted on this marriage;—for they *have* insisted on it, and of that I am certain. Alick would have been afraid to look a hardened London girl like Louisa Graham in the face, if she hadn't thrown dust into his eyes to blind him.'

'Love-powder, probably,' suggested Gerald, provokingly.

'Love-powder! nonsense! I tell you he was just as likely to fraternize with an hyena as with old Graham's daughter. If I had seen it going on I would have warned him of the snare they laid for him.'

'It would have done no earthly good,' said Clayton, coming towards his wife. 'When a man is running on to danger with the kind of impetus that love propels him with, you may as well attempt to stop a cannon, or a cricket-ball with *your* bare hand, my dear.'

'Well, it's very stupid, I know that,' said Flo; 'but tell me, Clayton, do you care to stop here longer? Gerald's so tiresome, and says the copper's stripped, or something, off the yacht.'

'Quite true,' responded Gerald, 'and I give you credit for remembering the complaint. It won't do for old Aylmer when he returns from Rio to find the "Madelina" disabled, so we must give her two days at least in dock.'

'And then?' inquired Florence.

'And then? Why, what do you say to cruizing round to Trinidad? It's the most beautiful of all the islands. And, after all, we needn't stay there longer than we like.'

The proposition met with unanimous approbation; and Florence lost no time in making a silent mental calculation of the chances for and against the mail from home arriving before *she* made good her departure from Jamaica. For she had spoken the truth in saying that she hated letters—hated them so, that had she but been given her choice she would have gone, for awhile at least, far from the haunts of civilized man, and even would have taken up her quarters in some

Gorilla-haunted country where the Queen's image upon paper is an unknown thing.

On the present occasion, the fates and the shipwrights all appeared to be in the interest of Florence Bernard, for in eight-and-forty hours the yacht was pronounced ready for sea; and on one moonlit evening they went on board of her, to be ready for departure on the morrow.

Their voyage to Trinidad was rendered slow by adverse winds; but Florence bore the aggravation calmly, since she expected to receive no letters at Port of Spain, their excursion thither not having been in contemplation when Clayton last wrote home to England.

It was a lovely early morning when the yacht, with her snow-white sails spread out to catch the breeze, entered the Grand Boras, which leads into the Gulf of Porca. To Gerald, who was well acquainted with the countries they were visiting, the duty usually fell to act as 'showman' to the party, and on this occasion, in right of his office, he insisted on Florence leaving her cabin to admire the beauty of the prospect.

'How beautiful!' exclaimed Florence, in the stereotyped words with which every tourist satisfies his or her *cicerone* that the wonders he expatiates on are appreciated. 'How very beautiful!'

And truly it was a scene beyond the praise of words! Close to the vessel, on the port side—so close, indeed, that they might have thrown a biscuit from the deck upon the land, arose the precipitous wooded shore of Trinidad, whilst, on looking over the starboard quarter, they could discern, and that very clearly, the dark blue mountains of the Spanish main. As they glided slowly forward on the still, calm waters, the scenery appeared to Florence as though it wore a very dream of beauty, so all unlike was it to anything that her eyes had ever rested on before. At the base of the rich and thickly-wooded acclivities stretched a sandy beach, by which the pale green sea was skirted; and every few hundred yards, in little nooks sheltered by Cocoa and Banama trees, they perceived pretty fishermen's huts simply built of mud and wattles, and thatched with the leaves of the Cacoa tree. Round and about these little tenements the nets of the owners were hanging up to dry, the small canoe being hauled up before each separate door, while little naked *blackies* were running here and there in all the wild enjoyment of their savage freedom. Proceeding onwards, and after passing these signs and symptoms of habitation, they came upon a wilder scene, for there, looking as if it had never been disturbed by hand or foot of man, were massive groves of the richest tropical vegetation, in the midst of which flourished tall and bright flowering Cacti, and various gigantic trees of whose names the sailor was totally ignorant, but whose branches were covered with gorgeous crimson flowers which almost dazzled the eye with the intensity of their lustre.

And now the gulf itself began to open to their view, in the shape of a glorious expanse of water, dotted here and there with tiny fishing-boats whose white sails glistened in the hot morning sun. To distinguish objects clearly at a distance towards the town of Port of Spain was impossible, on account of the vapoury veil so like a mist which hangs in early morning over the delicious scenery of the Tropics; but still some tall and tapering masts were dimly visible, which told them where the town and harbour lay.

Passing by this jungly region the yacht next glided slowly past a lovely valley between two lofty mountains, the which acclivities were varied with patches of the bright-green sugar-cane, and here and there with the tall chimneys of the boiling-houses, from which (for the crop-season had set in) there rose volumes of thick black smoke, which, despite the antagonistic circumstances of sunlight and situation, carried the mind back again to

Old England and its 'valley of a hundred fires.'

'Clayton,' said Florence softly, as she stood upon the deck with her arm linked within her husband's, 'Clayton, dear, let us live here always. It is as beautiful as fairy-land—more lovely than any dream. I am sure that I could be always happy here.'

'And England, love! and the country home which you once made me hope that you would learn to care for? *My* serious duties too; and—'

'You couldn't possibly have come at a jollier time,' exclaimed Gerald, rather judiciously breaking in upon his brother's list of reasons why Florence should, for once in her life, be contradicted; 'you are very fortunate in that, for if I remember rightly this is the race-meeting season, when there will be lots of balls, and no end of fun.'

'Fun and dancing, in such a climate!'

'Yes, indeed; and I have known them keep it up night after night for a week. You must be prepared to go through any amount of dining-out exertion too, for there is no limit to the hospitality of the Creole inhabitants of this island.'

They were now fast approaching the town, of which, however, but little could be seen, as it is hidden from the sight of those at sea by a fine avenue of trees which runs up the principal street parallel with the wharves. They came to an anchor about a mile from the shore, and the 'Madelina' was instantly surrounded by shore-boats, the owners of which kept up an incessant volley of abuse of each other, mingled with adjurations to every one on board to enter the individual little crazy craft which called him owner.

Wearied of the confinement of the yacht, Clayton and Gerald jumped into a boat which bore conspicuously the euphonious names of 'Penelope Ann,' and desired to be rowed on shore.

The crew consisted of two stout negroes clad in striped cotton trousers, and having on their woolly heads broad-brimmed Panama hats. They showed their great white teeth with grins of ineffable delight and triumph as they moved away with their prize, pulling to the nearest wharf with wild shouts, and as they appeared to Clayton, the most incomprehensible ejaculations.

Florence watched them as they left the vessel (for the purpose, Clayton told her, of discovering on shore some fitting place for her reception), and her dark eyes brimmed over with amusement as she caught a few words of flattery offered by the crafty crew.

'Pretty gen'l'man dat—eh?' said one to the other with a knowing wink at Clayton, and pronouncing the last interrogatory monosyllable with a kind of nasal grunt, which it is difficult to describe on paper.

'Berry glad to see him, a—a—a!' responded the joint owner of the 'Penelope Ann.' 'Berry glad to see him. He *too* pretty; 'spose he come for join de garrison. He Crimea hero, dat; what you say, Jack?'

The voices of the rowers died away in the distance, and Florence remained seated under the awning, and in her place of predilection, namely, between the open port-holes, taking advantage of every breath that blew across the water. She felt singularly light of heart that morning. She did not ask herself the reason why her 'bosom's soul should sit more lightly on its throne' just then; but lay there on her cushions with a luxurious sense of present enjoyment which she forebore to break by any foolish reasonings on the whys and wherefores of her great content.

She had taken very kindly to the sea, had Florence Bernard, and had proved herself, as Gerald said, a 'plucky one, and no fresh-water sailor,' on their lengthened voyage. She looked into the bright-green water now, as into a tried friend's face; and as the rippling wavelets washed against the vessel's sides, their voices seemed to speak to her of peace, and of the broad gulf which lay between her and her saddened memories—between her home upon the waters and the now hated land which she had left so far behind her.

There was a dreamy stillness in the air, which hushed her to repose—brought sleep, too, to her conscience, and whispered to her troubled spirit, 'Peace—be still.'

She took but little note of time during the lengthened absence of the little party on the shore, nor had she yet begun to weary of her solitude, when suddenly, and almost within hailing distance of the yacht, she saw the boat approaching her.

She raised the 'glass,' which lay within her reach, and scanned it towards the little craft which danced upon the waters gaily. She saw their faces quite distinctly—so distinctly that she could perceive that both looked graver (Gerald more especially) than when they had left the 'Madelina' two short hours before.

'What could be the reason of those lengthened faces?' Florence asked herself, as every oar-stroke brought their features into clearer view, and every moment showed her still more plainly that there was a gloomy shadow upon each.

Gerald, she could see, had one hand on the tiller, but in the other—ah, Heaven! what was it he held so carefully, as, with sailor-like dexterity, he steered the boat under the vessel's quarter? Surely they were not letters—English letters—letters from home that, as he stepped on deck, she saw in Captain Bernard's hand! Ah, yes, it was too true, that cruel, rapid surmise; and in a moment she—that woman who had lately hugged herself in a fancied security—trembled before what seemed to her a certain danger.

She sprung up eagerly to meet her husband, (and, it might be, to know her fate at once) as Clayton's head appeared above the gangway. There was no need for one who knew well every turn of that expressive face, to take a second look, for Florence saw at once, and by a single glance that *she* at least was safe.

'A letter for you, Florence, darling!' Bernard said, 'from Susan Brigham. Things look bad, we hear, for the poor prisoner, and,' he added, while an expression of exceeding pain passed over his handsome features, 'not over well, I greatly fear, for Marian Clavering. But read your letter, love. It may contain more cheerful matter than those which I have just been reading.'

She held the harmless-looking missive in her hand, and *could* not do his bidding. What if (she thought) his eyes should wander to the page, and he might see some word that would betray her secret? And yet she dared not seem to shrink from what that letter might contain; so she rose up, and murmuring something of the heat, and that she was very tired, went down the companion-ladder to her cabin.

It was late in the afternoon when Clayton Bernard, thinking that his wife's siesta had lasted long enough, knocked at her cabin door. She opened it at once, and to his surprise threw herself, without an uttered word, into his arms, and lay and sobbed upon his breast.

He tried to soothe her, but for long he tried in vain; but at last the gasps which shook her frame decreased in vehemence, and in the intervals between her short convulsive sobs she said, in a low, frightened voice—

'Clayton, my letter, too, was about poor Cousin Chrissy. Susan says that—that—perhaps they may condemn her—and—Oh! Clayton, think how dreadful—that she may be—'

But here her emotion choked her, and covering her face with her hands, she wept long and unrestrainedly.

He let her sorrow have its way, and when the burst of grief had moderated, she cried imploringly—

'Clayton, this must not be. Oh, no! a thousand times I would rather die than think of such an awful wrong and cruelty. You do not care to stay from England longer, dear,' she added. 'It would be the same to you, perhaps, to go home now, and I would so much rather.'

He gazed at her in speechless admiration. To think that she, who every day expressed her joy that the width of the broad Atlantic lay between her and England, should, for the sole wish to see and solace an afflicted woman, urge him to do the thing she hated! It was a new proof, had any more been wanting, of the exceeding beauty of her character, and of the wisdom of his choice.

He drew her closer to his breast, and kissed her fondly.

'Ever the same,' he murmured. 'Ever unselfish and tender-hearted. Your will is mine, my darling, and if you think that we can by our presence be of any use to Mrs. Fletcher or to Susan, let us not lose a day, but embark at once for England.'

And so it was arranged that it should be; and happily for the furthering of their plan, the steamer for St. Thomas's and thence to

England was to leave Port of Spain on the following day. In her they engaged their berths, and Florence, who had hurried on all the preparations for departure with a feverish haste, found herself within twenty-four hours of her arrival at Port of Spain, steaming out from the beauteous harbour, and bound for the country which she both hoped and dreaded to reach before the Spring Assizes, when Cousin Chrissy's fate was to be decided.

CHAPTER XVIII.

MR. DRIVER RECOLLECTS AN APPOINTMENT IN BELGRAVE SQUARE.

NEARLY two months have slipped away since Olive Bernard, sick, contrite, and dispirited, had come to crave the shelter of a home from Cousin Chrissy's god-daughter. Ostensibly, few changes affecting any of the actors in our story have taken place since that cold January night, when Olive's garbled tale awoke such pity for her sorrows, and moved the unsuspicious Susan to share her room, and even her nightly couch, with Clayton Bernard's sister-in-law. It was, indeed, a 'strange bedfellow' with which misery had made that pure young girl acquainted, and one whom Susan, had she known the whole, would probably have kept at greater distance. But even though such might have been the prudent counselling of her sober judgment, it would have been scarcely possible to obey its dictates, since Olive's state of health (as soon became apparent) was such as to render it impossible for her to leave the house. In that small lodging, therefore, she remained—not suffering from serious illness, but broken down apparently in nerves and constitution, and dragging on a weary life from day to day, and hour to hour.

It was in vain that Susan strove to rouse her to exertion—in vain that she appealed to every feeling which she felt a wife and an expectant mother might respond to. Nothing she urged had any weight with Olive, who sat through the long weary day beside the chimney-corner, in listless discontent and brooding melancholy.

The time of Cousin Chrissy's trial meanwhile had grown very near, and with its close approach the fears in Susan's heart outstripped her hopes, and made her almost dread the day which was to terminate that long suspense. The one true friend, above and far beyond the rest, who never for an hour failed her, was Ernest Audaine, and what the balm of his bright genial presence was to her all through that trying time was known to her own breast alone.

He is walking with her from the prison now, and speaking as he often did of Marian Clavering.

'It is most wonderful to me,' he said, 'how much you quiet women bear. I sometimes think if I had been a wife, and married to a brute like that, I should have resisted—left him—put the world between me and the man who outraged every feeling, wounded me in my most vulnerable point—and worse than all the rest, filled me with hourly shame when I remembered that I bore his name.'

'I do not wonder at your excitement,' Susan said, 'but habit, happily, has made your sister bear her trials with apparent patience. I never saw a cloud on Marian's face when *he* addressed her — as I have often heard him do—as if she were his slave, or spaniel. *I* should have been less patient, I am afraid, and forgotten the soft answer that turneth away wrath, in my indignation at his injustice and the rude, savage words he used.'

Before Ernest could respond to her remark, which he probably would have done by something more than acquiescence in its truth, they were surprised by the stopping exactly in front of them of a singular looking, dwarfish figure, who had come rapidly from the direction of Susan's lodging. He touched his hat in rather clownish fashion, and seemed to stand uneasily in one of Nichols's ready-made great coats—a coat that nearly trailed upon the ground, and hid his knuckles with its cotton-velvet cuffs.

'I beg your pardon, mem,' he said to Susan, mincingly, 'but there's a lady taken ill up there'—and he pointed high in air to Susan's attic, which, but for its exalted position, might be said to be at no great distance. 'She's taken very ill, and said I was to go for you. I knew you, mem, by sight, and took the liberty to speak.'

She had no notion who the speaker was, no more had Ernest. The moment also, and the news,—'Some one was taken ill!' Olive, of course—was not well calculated for conjecture or delay. She asked no questions therefore, but writing hastily a few words upon a card with pencil, put it into Audaine's hand.

'Hurry with it to the doctor, please,' she said. 'He lives close by. It is for Olive. She is—is near her time, poor thing, and—oh, Mr. Audaine!—tell him to send a nurse—and—'

She stopped, in speech at least, though still she hurried on towards the humble haberdasher's shop, far above which, and at the topmost story, poor Olive lay alone in her great mortal suffering.

Susan was far too frightened for her friend to choose her words, or even to remember, when she made a confidant of Ernest, that he, a single and a 'fashionable' man, was hardly an appropriate messenger to send on such an errand. Of this he seemed to be to the full as oblivious as she was herself, for only waiting to shake hands, and promise haste and help, he ran rather than walked in the direction she had pointed out.

And now, leaving for awhile the inexperienced young woman, whose work appeared extremely likely to increase rapidly upon her hands, we must follow Amelius Driver in his slower course along the street which Ernest trod with such gigantic strides before him.

'There goes the swell!' he muttered to himself, as, secure in the perfect arrangement of his toilette, he strutted on, convinced that the stares of passers-by arose either from their envy of, or their admiration for, his fashionable appearance. 'There goes the swell; Lord, how fat those fellows cut it! He's spooning that there gurl, I reckon. Lawks, what fun! and how confounded blue he'll look when he finds out her cousin's not the Earl, and that—' But here his soliloquy was cut short by an aggressive butcher's boy, who, with his tray upon his shoulder, was evidently inciting another street acquaintance, endowed apparently like himself with a keen sense of the ridiculous, to 'poke fun' at Master Driver.

'I say, Jem, ain't he got a 'at on? that's all!' said he of the blue cotton garment, appealing to his friend in fustian.

'We could put our two 'eds inside of it, we could,' grinned Jem, approvingly. 'I say, Bill, don't you tread upon his coat-tails. Where's six-foot-'igh, I wonders, what ought to be a t'other side of it.'

They were close behind, those two tormentors of the indignant Yussy, who (for his disposition was, as has been shown, rather of an irascible order) turned round upon them with a crimson face of passion.

'I say, you chaps, move on—don't you be imperent now, or I shall call for the police.'

The lads burst into a simultaneous roar of derisive laughter.

'I say, don't you try it on now—don't you go to waste your precious time at the perlice hoffice; you go and meet your fancy-gurl, as is a waiting for you in the Park—'

'With a bucket of flowers to stick in yer buzzom,' put in Jem.

'And a kiss for yer lips, old fellar. My eyes! how jolly good. I say, what'll you give us not to tell about the other gurl—the one that's round the corner?'

What reply the exasperated Yussy might, under more propitious circumstances, and with fewer odds against him, have made to such unseemly chaffing, must for ever remain a subject for conjecture, as, at that critical moment, a Hansom cab—fortunately an empty one—passed along the street, which Yussy, recollecting that discretion is the better part of valour, prudently hailed. He jumped in, and turning round after he was seated at the *gamins*, whose numbers were now (so rapid is the accumulation of a crowd) beginning to multiply, he shook his fist towards them menacingly.

There was a derisive shout from the street boys as Yussy drove away, which shout was unpleasantly accompanied by sundry pieces of advice adapted to his costume and appearance generally, which Master Amelius fondly hoped had escaped the notice of his driver.

It was a good horse (or rather had in its day been one) which conveyed Amelius Driver at a swinging trot away from Clerkenwell, and in a south-westerly direction from that dreary neighbourhood. He had an appointment to keep at 2 P.M.—an appointment (oh, that those 'little villains' had but known it!) with a great lord—a lord that gave him money—thought no end of *him*—Amelius. 'I should rather think so,' mused the excited youth, as delighted with the rapid motion, he bowled along towards Belgrave Square.

But to account for Master Driver's exultation, it is necessary to go back for one week in our story, and recount certain events that had taken place in the West-end of London during that rather eventful period.

CHAPTER XIX.

LORD ASHINGTON IN A FIX.

For some cause or other—no one seemed to inquire what, or who was at the bottom of the delay—but for some unexplained cause the marriage of Alick Harley with Miss Louisa Graham had not yet, as the saying is, 'come off.' That it was still 'going on' was evident from the fact that the betrothed lovers were always seen together both in public and in private, and from the no less unquestionable proof that the *trousseau* was in full progress of manufacture, the carriage standing in the lustre of its new varnish at the coach-maker's, and that presents were pouring in from all quarters for the future Countess.

Alick's education for the world during his

two months of schooling had gone on prosperously enough. He seldom felt painfully shy now; never, indeed, excepting when with Lady Annabella or Sir Carleton, both of whom habitually sneered at and snubbed him. Had he been of a less submissive nature, and of a bolder, higher spirit, they would have been more careful how they tried him so; for the breaking off of such a match was not to be lightly hazarded, and as a son-in-law—a patient, liberally-disposed, and grateful son-in-law—Lady Annabella never doubted but that Mr. Harley would prove himself eventually invaluable. But with all these convictions of Alick's great importance to the family's well-being, the heads of that family often found it difficult, from habit and constitutional temperament, to avoid making themselves extremely disagreeable to the future Earl of Ashington. It was their nature to be unpleasant—they could hardly help it. They were disagreeable, coarse, unfeeling, and regardless both of their own good manners and of other people's feelings, even when their intentions were at their best, and those they desired to propitiate were dwellers in high places, and of the number of those on whom the world of fashion had set its seal of approbation. But if Alick's future relations had the happy knack of leaving a bad impression on the minds of those whose good opinions they desired to gain, how much the more must the influence of their innate unpleasantness (may I be allowed the word?) have been felt by the large majority, namely, those whom they did not feel inclined to conciliate, or whose sensitive vanity they delighted to wound.

Besides, Lady Annabella had boasted that she would make Mr. Harley what she called *presentable*,—would teach him the great use of words for purposes of concealment, and that to 'smile, and smile, and smile,' and be a hypocrite, was an essential accomplishment in the world which he would live in. To say that Alick thoroughly enjoyed himself during the process of transformation into that artificial state of being would be untrue, for he was about as happy as a sick elderly gentleman enduring embellishment in the chair of a fashionable dentist, or as a hitherto neglected poodle-dog who finds himself suddenly condemned to the tender mercies of the tonsor's razor. But however small had been the amount of pleasure he could tax his memory with enjoying during those weeks of rather unsatisfactory courtship, Alick Harley had made considerable progress in knowledge of the world under the tutorship of his able instructors. He had learned, too, thoroughly to appreciate the luxuries which he now daily indulged in; and looking back with pity on himself in his old Curate days of toil and hardship, he could give his *equals* in the Park and ball-room an off-hand nod of familiar recognition, while for humbler old acquaintances he would vouchsafe only one feebly-offered finger to prove that memory of the past had not as yet completely left her seat. He had some pangs of conscience at the commencement of his throwing off the 'slough' of his old better self; but in a Sybaritish life a conscience soon seers over, and the once humble Curate held his head aloft, save, as I said before, when Lady Annabella (metaphorically speaking) 'bonnetted' him, or, worse misfortune still, when Ernest Audaine fixed his calm, searching eyes upon his altered friend reproachfully.

It was in the early days of March, and half the world had come to town for the short pre-season which Palm Sunday puts an end to, when Lord Ashington, who had been suffering from that worse than bugbear to the old, called 'influenza,' was sitting, cross and feeble, in the small library of his grand town-house. The sun was hot without, and already a green tinge was faintly laid by Nature's hand upon the thorns and lilac-trees. Spring was coming—that was very clear outside the windows; but within the rich man's lordly home there was still winter—a winter of discontent and peevishness—a winter of old age, white hair, and deepening wrinkles. He had been sitting in his cushioned velvet chair since luncheon time alone, and four had struck some minutes past upon the alabaster clock (which told its tale of passing time as softly as a courtier's voice, upon the chimney-piece. The Earl moved on his easy seat with restless irritability. He had the newspaper spread out upon his knees, but, for all the information he could glean from it, the journal might as well have stayed within the newsman's shop, for the old eyes that rested longingly upon its columns were dimmed by recent sickness, and the small letters of the printed sheet seemed one great blot before his weakened vision.

'I wonder what on earth keeps Harley out so late?' soliloquized the lonely man, who wanted Alick's eyes and tongue to make up for his own deficiencies. 'Riding, of course, with that confounded woman! Women are nuisances at all times, always in the way—always—'

But here his ungallant as well as ungrateful soliloquy was interrupted by the noiseless entry of his valet, who placed before his eyes a shabby-looking card, saying that a person (he could not bring himself to say a gentleman!) begged to be allowed—this was the term given to the request by the obsequious serving-man—to have a few minutes' conversation with his Lordship.

His Lordship, on hearing this remarkable instance of audacity, opened his eyes as wide as the effects of his late disorder would allow of, and stared wonderingly at the audacious messenger.

The angry, frowning face was so speakingly indicative of the strongest description of dissent, that words were needless; nevertheless, the valet, who had probably received a 'sop' to soften his relentless nature, ventured to urge the claims of the strange person on his lordship's notice.

'He looks a decent man, my lord,' he said, 'and bade me say a name he thought your lordship would remember. He said, my lord, as it was Hopgood, and that the lawyer, Mr. Bracebridge, knew about it.'

The room was very dark (considering how light it was outside) for the green blinds were drawn before the windows; but dark although it was, the servant saw the change that came over his master's face, and commented upon it in the after-days when great convulsions shook the mighty house of Harley to its centre.

'What sort of fellow does he seem?' asked his lordship, turning his back towards the valet and speaking in a voice that trembled slightly—'A poor man? One that's come to beg? Ask him—no, don't—I'll see him for a moment—bring him in.'

The servant, who had not expected so ready an acquiescence, soon returned, ushering in a man of middle age, whom Lord Ashington perceived at a single glance was a stranger to him. There was not a shadow of embarrassment perceptible in the round dark eyes that almost seem to glare beneath their shaggy eyebrows as they fixed themselves tenaciously upon the old peer's face, and seemed to fascinate him by their magnetic influence. It was not a pleasant face, and Lord Ashington, as he took in the angry lines and darkened brow, half wished, although he was no coward, that Harris had been told to stay behind the door.

Redfern (for it was he who had intruded in so unceremonious a manner on that sacred privacy) had removed his hat—although with no respectful intention — on his entrance. He had no wish to bow before the wealth and rank that niched itself within that gilded chamber, but his head burned with fever, and the dew pearled upon his low, broad brow, making all covering an oppression to him.

'You desired to speak to me on business, sir, I heard,' began Lord Ashington, who was habitually courteous to his inferiors, more so infinitely than to his equals. 'I am rather unwell to-day, and must request you to be quick with what you have to say. Pray be seated,' and he pointed to a chair which stood at some little distance from his own, and at the other side of the small writing-table on which his arm was resting.

Redfern took the offered seat, and then said in a loud, harsh voice, which sounded very like impertinent familiarity to the great man's ears—

'I am come, Lord Ashington, to speak my mind out to you at last. I've been a long time thinking of it—a deuced long time thinking of it, but it's none the worse for that, but, on the contrary, I've got a string of pleasant things to say which I hadn't the good luck to know of before this.'

He paused to wipe his forehead with a red and yellow snuffy handkerchief, the which he threw into the greasy hat that lay upon the great Earl's papers.

The latter drew himself up with an air of most exceeding dignity.

'Sir,' he said, 'this is a liberty—and—and—a manner of speaking which I cannot permit, and I must request that you will leave the room immediately.'

He laid his hand upon the bell-rope, but Redfern had foreseen the movement, and quicker than thought seized the Earl's feeble fingers in his iron grasp.

'Coward and villain!' he hissed out between his firm set teeth. 'You thought to call your servants to the rescue, did you? You thought to make them turn me out into the street! I who have come for vengeance—I who have come to hurl the name of Edith Hopgood in your teeth—the name of Edith whom you ruined—blighted with your foul passion! And then—' and as he spoke he shook the aged form of the infirm old man in his wild, desperate passion—'married her to an honest man—you base, depraved old sinner—you miserable and most accursed cheat that ever dared to call himself a gentleman!'

How long in his blind rage he would have heaped invective on the aristocratic head that vibrated beneath his clutching fingers, who can say? Neither did he know himself the reason why, then and there, he did not shake the life out of that resistless frame, and send the old man's soul, with all its weight of unrepented guilt, into the world beyond the grave.

But something—it was not pity, surely, but rather an instinctive fear for his own safety—stayed his hand, and letting go his hold, he propped his frightened enemy against the velvet of his comfortable chair, and held him there.

END OF VOL. II.

CPSIA information can be obtained
at www.ICGtesting.com
Printed in the USA
LVHW040435110522
718423LV00002B/326

9 783375 002107